Rose Mulready's short fiction has appeared in various publications, including *HQ* magazine and the *Sleepers Almanac*s. Her novel *The Day We Lost the Moon* was shortlisted for the 2012 Victorian Premier's Literary Award for an Unpublished Manuscript.

She is The Australian Ballet's Content Expert, and lives in Melbourne, by the sea.

rosemulready.wordpress.com

THE BONOBO'S DREAM

ROSE MULREADY

First published in Seizure by Xoum in 2016

Xoum Publishing
PO Box Q324, QVB Post Office,
NSW 1230, Australia

www.seizureonline.com
www.xoum.com.au

ISBN 978-1-925143-24-9 (print)
ISBN 978-1-925143-25-6 (digital)

Cataloguing-in-publication data is available from the National
Library of Australia

Internal design and typesetting © Xoum Publishing 2015

Cover design by David Henley
Cover illustration by Sam Paine, www.sampaine.com
Printed in Australia by McPherson's Printing Group

Edited by Tom Langshaw

*Viva La Novella 4 was made possible through the generous support of
Xoum Publishing, IPED and the NSW Society of Editors.*

To advance the
profession of editing

To my Storybook Cat, and the Great State of Iowa

PART ONE: FISHBOWL

1

The birch is a quiet tree. It listens.

James sits by the window, touching the glass lightly. He has just taken off his drawing harness. The finished sketch lies on the desk: it is of the birch trees, pale and precise in the silver air. A daffodil at their feet is the only colour. Ruffled, a golden face staring.

He puts one finger in his mouth, tasting the glass.

'You are listening. Aren't you?' he says to the trees.

Receives their silence.

His goldfish sing in their bowl. The morning is ripening. He goes over to the thank-you-jeeves and takes out his shorts. Today will be full of fighting, he knows. His mother will scream. Whenever Charity comes there is always fighting. That's why he wishes she would stay away, even though she always brings him a present, kisses him, holds him close so he smells her sharp scent.

And today it's her birthday. It's always worse on her birthday.

He dresses in yellow, the shorts and the T-shirt with the reindeer. The T-shirt smells clean. He buries his nose in it.

Clean.

There is a fumbling at the door. He watches the handle turn.

'James?'

Sighing a little, he straightens the reindeer just so on his chest.

'Yes?'

Suzanne comes into the room, wanders to the window, peers accusingly at the sky. Her hair is askew. She smells of cigarettes.

She picks up the drawing from the desk, sniffs, lets it drop.

'It's good.'

'Thanks.'

She fingers the harness.

'This is getting too small for you.'

'It's fine. Don't worry about it.'

'James, you have to learn that you grow out of things. You have to learn to let go.'

'I will,' he says quickly.

She gazes at him, the harness held loosely in her hands. He looks down at the carpet. Thick, hushed, the colour of bone. His toes sink into it, and are gone.

'Look at me.'

Her face reminds him of the daffodil – blank and

open, staring, too bright. He can smell her. She smells of her morning dose. Powdery, faintly metallic.

'James,' she says softly, 'do you love me?'

'Yes,' he whispers. His throat skins over, a familiar mechanism to block tears.

'Do you love Suzanne? Do you love your mother?'

'Yes.'

'Really? *Really* love me? Forever?'

'Forever.'

She walks to his dresser and taps her long finger-nails against the glass of his goldfish bowl. The fish rise eagerly, singing in high, frantic voices. She stares into their mouthing faces.

He swallows. 'If you do that you have to give them powder. They think you're going to feed them. That's what I do when I feed them.'

She turns on him. 'So what, sweetie? So what?'

He inhales, exhales. 'They think you're going to feed them, so you have to give them their powder.'

'I don't *have* to do anything, *p'tit*. I don't have to do a damn thing.'

The fish clamour in four-part harmony. It's like a knife in him, twisting.

'I mean,' and she laughs her low husky laugh, the one that means *whatever*, 'you talk as if they're real.'

The singing, singing, singing.

Her lips livid and puffed from the dose.

He begins to talk to himself inside his head: *Reindeer, I love you reindeer, reindeer protect my chest, bright yellow protect me, birch trees, hear me, hear me.*

And they must hear because she shrugs and wanders out of his room, running her hands over the things on his dresser and his bedside table, lingering to peer again at the sky, turning to give him a long look from half-closed lids, leaning for a little against the door, then shutting it after herself with a small, deliberate click.

The air settles to stillness.

The fish croon hopelessly.

He goes to his dresser and gets out their powder and they carol gaily at the sight of it but his hands are shaking so much that most of it goes over the floor and they gulp up what they can and then spiral down to the bottom of the bowl and lurk there, half hidden in their weeds.

2

I t gets harder every year.

Aquila lowers himself into the sunken tub, making small sounds of pain and complaint. His whole back burns from the sculpture harness. He suspects he is developing an allergy to the polymer. His heart is fluttering weakly, his lungs turning themselves inside out like blown umbrellas.

Umbrella, he murmurs to himself. The word is meaningless now, an anachronism. It could be the name of a princess. A princess with no kingdom.

The water takes him kindly. 'Hotter,' he says, and the temperature dial reddens. 'Hotter, hotter, hotter,' he says, closing his eyes, his head lolling, 'hotter,' until the autoregulator kicks in and says, softly, sweetly, 'That's hot enough, don't you think?'

His muscles unknot in a slow, painful progression. He waits for the dose to come on. Lately it seems to be getting longer and longer, but he knows better than to increase it. Doesn't want to end up in the clinic having his neurons resensitised. Doesn't want to leave the house, in fact. Not anymore.

He thinks about the piece he's been working on, sitting in the basement. Crouched there. He made it, but it scares him. Not least because it may not sell, not even with his name. And then what. He has expenses, a whole stack of them. Wife, kids, costly and demanding mistress.

When he closes his eyes, he still sees the ceiling, a resin transfer of *Hive*, his most famous work. (Or one of them. Academics and fans argue over the comparative merit of this or that masterpiece.) *Hive*, a universal favourite, is a hatched dome of greens that, with the appropriate dose, 'prods the neurons into an unprecedented lattice of tranquillity, a holy calm' (*toploft* magazine). Hence its presence in his bathroom, where he comes to put himself back together after the rigours of harness-time, where he comes to be reborn.

Come on, dose, beautiful dose, come.

When he was young . . . in his prime . . . he wouldn't be lying in a bath like an old woman to wind down after a session. No, he'd be screwing the peachy ass off some groupie, or even, in those days, Suzanne. He'd strap on the harness like a warrior of old and dash off some incomparable, dazzling piece that would sell for a quarter million, then shower sleekly and go out to the cloud bars. In the best ones he had his own table on permanent reserve, in subtly secluded alcoves – not so hidden as to disguise his presence (after all, half the dupes in the place were there to ogle him and whatever five-star princess he had on his arm that night, to steal long envious glances at whatever rollicking good time they were having), but discreet enough to allow the moments of privacy that became necessary over the course of a standard evening.

And the views. Pristine ringside views of the night sky, its carefully choreographed comets, its skilfully arranged constellations. Once, on his thirtieth birthday, they made one in the shape of his face. The maître d' presented it like a gift, whisking away a gauze curtain to reveal the tribute, *ooh*s and *ahh*s all round, but he found it eerie – his face snared there in its own radiance, cold and huge and haughty. Hanging in the dark sky. All during that riotous night he could dent (ever so slightly) the monumental buzz he had on, just by catching his own glittering eye.

He hasn't been to the city in months. He's stopped buying the news. Down to one girl (not counting, as he doesn't, Suzanne). One girl, and he can barely be bothered to do her. Despite her incontrovertible, raraavis sexiness. Despite her semi-constant demands that he should.

When he opens his eyes and sees the ash-green resins and blond pine and concave mirrors of the bathroom lift and settle into a subtly different configuration, glowing softly, he knows the dose has kicked. He tips his head back, sighing, and takes a long look at *Hive*.

This house that his talent has built, its pitch-perfect

elegance, its airy greens and creams, its walls of glass admitting views of delicate Nordic forest, its cloud-soft carpets and linens, the dulcet voices of its appliances, this *calm*. No wonder he doesn't want to leave it. This house that his talent has built, that he has wrested into being, like a god creating his own sweet goddess out of clay. This peerless shell.

He loves it in long pulses, his throat bared to the ceiling.

Aquila.

Aquila.

The phone is calling him in murmurs. A sound like ebbing waves. He turns his head reluctantly and waves at the lens. Like everything else in the house it is meticulously styled, fashioned like pooled mercury, hanging on the wall like the cocoon of some high-sheened insect. It clears to show the caller.

It's Antoinette. She says nothing, merely bares a breast, licks a finger and runs it over the nipple. He looks, says nothing. She shrugs and the lens thickens to silver.

Antoinette, now there's a woman. Twenty years younger than him, twenty times the libido, quite the temper – she once attacked him with a fork after he criticised her new wall hangings. Superbly black, with peacock-blue nipples engineered by Cavielleri himself. She collects, not art, but artists. He's given her precious little encouragement, what with one thing and another, but she's persistent. Tenacious. He's worth a lot to her. She will call back and back and back until he agrees to meet her. But not in the city. He's done with the city, the news. She can meet him in the Meadows: so impeccable a hotel that it's almost like he's never left home. And it's only a short catazoom's ride away. She will complain, of course. She will perhaps rant a little. But in the end, she will agree.

'Hotter.'

The bath gushes willingly. He stretches, testing the taut elastic of his muscles. The aches are gone, replaced by a lionish feeling of pent strength. He feels a colossus, or near enough. He glances fondly at *Hive*.

He is a genius. He really is. They say it, and it's true. He's a public treasure. The world would be littler, colder without him. Lives would be dimmer. He is that rare thing, a master. As rare as comets used to be.

His every pore feels luminous.

That thing in the basement. First sculpture he's done in a long time. He hadn't known he was going to do it. Came out of nowhere. Nothing like his usual work. Like something done by someone else. It worries him, a little. Not a lot. It will sell, his things always sell.

He waves lazily in the direction of the lens.

'Heide,' he tells it.

The phone says 'Certainly, Aquila,' and the lens clears to show his dealer's face, turning towards him in surprise. He hasn't contacted her in weeks, although she has been calling daily, asking about the new work.

'Heide, how are you? You're looking great, just great.'

'Thanks. You do know that you're naked?'

He dismisses this with a lordly gesture. 'Look, Heide, I finished the work.'

Her face brightens.

'You've finished? Really? Can I see it? Oh God, you have no idea of the calls I've been fielding. We're out of stock, we really need to position it now, this week if possible. Is that possible? Have you transferred the membrane?'

Heide – a thin, gingerish redhead – reminds him, in this eager mood, of a rabbit.

'Well, dear, there's just one thing. It's not a painting. It's a sculpture.'

She considers this. 'That could work. I mean, of course it will work. It'll price some of the lower-end buyers out of the market, and it won't be suitable for every home, but then, there are people out there who would rebuild their homes to accommodate your pieces. Remember Chaginoff built a whole new wing to house *Stamen*. Weng Fa did the same thing for *Polypop*.'

'This is a little different. A different direction for me.'

She frowns a little. 'Different? Different how?'

'You'll really just have to see it.'

'So, show me! I'm dying to see it, just dying.'

He hesitates. 'Right now I'm in the bath. It was a hell of a piece to get done. Sculpture's much harder on the body than painting. I need to relax.'

'Tonight?'

'Tonight's Charity's birthday. She's coming round for dinner.'

Heide's face, in the fish-eye enlargement of the lens, creases subtly with distaste.

'How is she?'

'She's never at her calmest this close to the start of the season. Her birthdays are always, shall we say, a trial.'

'I can only just picture.'

'I'm not sure that you can.'

The bath is cooling around him.

'Heide, I'm going to get out of this water. Let's spare your blushes and cut this short. I just wanted to let you know that I'm done. I'll show it to you tomorrow.'

'I can't wait, Aquila!'

And she means it. She really does.

The lens clouds and he steps out of the bath. He feels alert and hungry. Perhaps some breakfast, now. The towel feels gratifyingly textured against his skin.

Aquila, Aquila. The hushing waves of the phone.

It's Antoinette, and this time she's mad.

'Look, *chien*, do you know how many men I had last night?'

'No, but you can tell me, if you like.' He wraps the towel briskly around his hips.

Her nostrils flare to their fullest. 'Yes, I would very much like to tell you, *cochon*. There were nine. Each one of them was at least twenty years younger than you. Each one was more beautiful, had smoother skin, a bigger cock, better conversation. I came and came and came like I had never come before. Do you hear that, old man?'

'Well, pet, I'm very happy for you.'

'Cochon!'

'Listen, Antoinette, I've been working all night. I have to get some breakfast.'

'Fine. Go have *breakfast* with your zombie-crone wife.' She pulls her shirt open, flaunting for a moment her iridescent tits, before the lens darkens.

Spare him these turbulent women, wanting and wanting and wanting him.

He thinks he would rather like a chat with his son. He hasn't spent much time with him recently; the piece has kept him up late each night, and it's been a while since he made an appearance at the breakfast table. He pulls the towel from his hips and glances into one of the long mirrors as he smooths back his hair.

Funny, he looks better today, younger. As if that piece in the basement had been a disease leeching him, something he'd cut out to save himself.

He looks into his own eyes, remembering the moment when the maître d' had flung aside the curtain and everyone had gasped and clapped and whistled, everyone but him, staring at his glittering self in the empty sky.

3

Suzanne is in the kitchen, taking food from the smart waiter. With her back to him she still looks pretty good, shaggy blonde hair up in a rough twist and an ass that's holding its own (with a little help, granted, but who doesn't take a little help these days?). It's her face that has changed. Her skin is ashy, sallow, her eyes focused slyly on some unknowable distant thing. She stands with a foodshake in her hand, staring into the smart waiter. She often does this nowadays – stops what she's doing for no reason, as if she's noticed something.

'Is that for me?'

She jumps. 'No. I'm supposed to know you'll be at breakfast? There are berries. Oatcakes. You can have them. You've had your dose?'

'Of course. Where's James?'

She looks confused.

'James,' he says.

'He's coming. He's on his way.'

He spoons berries into a bowl. She takes a sip from the foodshake.

'Is everything done for tonight?'

She shrugs. 'I've ordered dinner, set the decorations.'

'What colours did you choose?'

'Silver. Dark red in the corners, the architraves. A kind of a bluebell colour for the table. Does that meet with the master's approval?'

He smiles blandly at her. 'As long as it meets with Charity's approval.'

There is something very fascinating, apparently, in the bottom of Suzanne's foodshake.

'You will try, this time?' he says. 'I'm not in the mood for a scene.'

'When were any of us ever in the mood for one of her scenes?'

'You provoke her.'

'She's an avalanche,' Suzanne says. 'She's a land-mine. You only have to walk near her.'

'Then don't walk near her. Stay in the safe valleys. On the safe roads.'

'How, precisely, does one do that? On her birthday? So close to the season? Have you ever managed to do that?'

'I don't flare up at her the way you do.'

'I don't *flare up!*'

'God, Suzanne. Listen to yourself. Have some irony, at least.'

'I had some irony, honey, but it was sucked out

during my last ass job and now I just have you.'

Their eyes meet for a long moment over the table. If someone walked in now, he thinks, and saw them, they would look like a couple in love.

And perhaps, in a kind of a way, they are.

'You have a bite on your neck,' she observes.

'The harness. It's been rubbing. It's the rub marks.'

'It looks like a bite.'

'They do sometimes.'

She appears to lose interest, holds up a berry by the stalk, observes its red glow against the light.

'You know James has been having dreams again,' she says.

'I told you that was just his imagination. His nonsense.'

'Yes, you did.'

'He's having his dose, isn't he?'

'Every morning.'

'And before bed?'

'Of course.'

'Then it's not possible.'

Suzanne considers the berry. 'It's not . . . desirable.'

The kitchen hums to itself, busy with its tasks; he takes a breath of air, savouring its even temperature. 'James plays at having dreams. It's a game, a fancy. The dose doctors say there are no exceptions. It's simple brain chemistry.'

'There's nothing simple about brain chemistry, as you of all people should know.'

Again the look between them, like love.

'James doesn't play,' says Suzanne. 'He dreams.'

'How do you know?'

'Sometimes I go in there.'

'And?'

'I see him asleep. But talking, talking to someone in a low steady voice.'

'He's pretending to be asleep.'

'Why would he do that?'

'He doesn't like you in his room. Haven't you ever noticed that?'

She sits back, puts the berry down.

'He likes it. He loves it.'

'No, he doesn't.'

'How would you know what he likes and doesn't?'

'I know. I know him. I don't need to spy on him.'

'I'm his *mother*,' she hisses.

'Yes.'

'Mothers don't spy.'

'That's exactly what they do. They do it all the time – especially to the boy children, the ones they don't understand.'

'Did you spy on Charity? Did you understand her?'

'Enough,' he says. He goes to the smart waiter, riffles through it and chooses an oatcake, though he's no longer hungry.

Suzanne cups her face: still strong-boned, still forthright and elegant, but somehow ruined, like a good house rotted to its foundations. 'I hear him,' she whispers. 'When I'm in his room. He talks. But he's asleep.'

'What does he say?'

Suzanne looks behind him, to the doorway.

'James.'

Aquila swings around. James is leaning in the doorway, arms folded sullenly over his chest. His clothes are a sulphurous yellow, a bright colour like egg yolk. His feet are bare.

'Want some breakfast?' Aquila says. He feels brimful of the complicated love James produces in him, a feeling that the boy is breakable, a feeling that he himself is dumb and lumbering as a bear, might snatch him up (as he longs sometimes to do) and in doing so snap something, not bones necessarily but some fragile reserve that his son requires.

'No, thanks. Just tea.'

'Tea? Since when do you drink tea?'

'Since forever,' James says, his gaze steady.

'It's true,' murmurs Suzanne.

'You can't just have tea.'

'I do all the time.'

Aquila turns on Suzanne, who shrugs irritably. 'As long as he's had his dose, and drinks a foodshake. What does it matter?'

'He should eat properly.'

'And what is that?'

'Like humans are supposed to eat. Designed to eat. With colours, textures, something to resist the teeth.'

Suzanne gives an amused snort and crushes the berry between her fingers. A small sigh of air escapes it.

'That's rubbish and you know it. All of this food is just pretty decoration. The foodshake is what counts.'

She pushes over her hardly touched shake to James, who fiddles with the straw for a moment then goes to the smart waiter, returning with leaves and a pot.

'It's important,' Aquila says. 'Our bodies were meant to –'

'Our bodies were meant to do all kinds of things.'

His son pours the tea through a strainer, taps the strainer a few times, lays it in the saucer and picks up the cup, watching him and Suzanne over the rim. The cup is yellow, part of a set Aquila ordered to go with the house, a pale, clear yellow like the winter sun that shines perpetually on the birch trees. For a moment James seems to glow from the reflection of the china on his near-transparent skin.

'Did you sleep well?' Aquila says.

James shrugs. 'What is well?'

'Did you wake up? Did you –'

'Leave him alone, Aquila.'

'Why? What's the matter?'

'Leave him *alone*. He's drinking his tea.'

'I'm drinking my tea,' says James.

'You're eight years old. Who drinks tea when they're eight years old?'

'I do.'

Suzanne hands James a lemon. He cuts it and squeezes; it makes two precise hisses of air. James stirs the tea, chinking the cup hardly at all, and looks down into the tiny vortex he's made. His head on his white slender neck is big as a dandelion, heavy with his thick red-blond hair.

'Can I go to my room now?'

'What for?' says Suzanne.

'I want to draw.'

'You've drawn already today.'

'I want to do another one.'

'We have the party tonight. You shouldn't get too tired.'

Aquila snaps an oatcake briskly in two.

'If he wants to draw, let him. When I was his age I drew and drew and drew. I was barely out of my harness.'

James looks up, and Aquila says, 'What did you draw today?'

'Trees.'

'What kind of trees?'

'Birches. The ones from my window.'

'It was very good,' offers Suzanne.

'I'm sure. Go and draw, if you want to, James.' He puts a hand to the child's face, just the backs of his fingers, and James leans against him briefly before leaving the room.

Suzanne gathers the tea things and shoves them willy-nilly into the smart waiter. 'That harness. It's too small for him. I think it may be – rubbing him.'

He sweeps the remains of the oatcake onto a plate and throws it in the smart waiter. This close to Suzanne, he can smell her cosmetics, powder-dry.

'I think it may be making him ill,' she whispers. 'That harness.'

'Rubbish,' he says. The dishes erase themselves. The kitchen clock chimes sweetly, human voices saying 'Nine.'

4

And someone inevitably asks her, where did you meet?

She tells a different story every time, one of her small, unnoticed rebellions.

Are they listening to her at all, these journalists, these patrons, these dealers, his girlfriends, his fans?

Not really. They're looking at her, thinking, *She's not that much, she's not anything, I wonder why he chose her, I wonder what he sees.*

'Must be good in bed.' A couple of them even say that to her. 'You must give great head.'

'Of course,' she says, and tosses her hair back, and drains her drink.

She does, of course. Given the chance. Doesn't she? He used to think so, or say so. But wait. Isn't it something more that makes a great artist choose you, bed you, plant you with his children, live by your side?

Or is it luck? Sheer blind luck of the moment? Roll of the dice? Happened to be there on the right morning, say the right word, the one that bound her to him, in a kind of a way, forever?

And she doesn't even know what it was. That dangerous word.

The kitchen is full of voices. The smart waiter announcing itself smugly. 'Breakfast!' 'Dishes!' The clock eulogising the hour. The menu reciting itself. The dose singing from its saucer.

'Aquila, Suzanne, James.'

It calls them all from the burnished glass dose-maid that opens, every morning, like a willing clam, like a flower. She hears it even through sleep, she wakes to hear it. She is always the first to answer its call.

There is so much she forgets these days. She is always pausing, right in the middle of something, to try and remember.

Where did you meet?

Yes, where?

She can only remember the stories she's made up.

At a cloud bar. He took me to his private booth. Like all the other girls. Except I wasn't like all the other girls.

I was the model for Houri. *He chained me to his wrist for nine days.*

I said to him . . .

He asked me to . . .

She never mentions the Old Quarter. Not once. What's true, anymore? Does she remember giving birth to Charity? Maybe. Remember giving birth to James? No.

Are they my children, really? Do they really love me? Should they? I don't remember. I don't remember.

I don't remember anything.

She stops these days, stops dead in her tracks (and what are these, her tracks? Where is she going, this train to the dead end of nowhere?), and tries, tries, tries to remember, to feel, to feel herself.

Before the next dose.

Who designed her mind?

How long has she been here?

How did they meet?

He found me in his pocket, in his gift bag, in his cake.

Was there a wedding? Weddings are out of fashion now, but she seems to remember one. Promises, her dress (*bad form, bad taste*), a thumb on her forehead, smelling of animal fat, his hand on her thigh.

Did she make this up?

Did she make all of this up – the graceful house with its useful voices, the views of birches? Before Aquila, what was there? Where does she come from?

She remembers the Old Quarter. The coming of fire.

She floats through the days like a shining, squeaking, nearly popping balloon and she never comes down. What kind of berries did she used to eat? Different to these. When you squeezed them they bled juice. Logan, blue, cloud. Cloudberry, the rarest. Food that fed you, before food became a decoration, a toy. Sky, and beneath it, trees.

One of their first times in bed. She wishes she could not remember. That time, the scent of it,

Magnolia grandiflora. A tree now dead, not even replicated. Magnolia, the first tree ever to flower, in the ancient forest. There outside their window. Blossoming desperately, spilling its scent, like ham and flower mixed, mingling with the scent of sex, like ham and flower mixed.

Does he remember?

She often wonders this. As she washes herself with Sente Sente DaisyLinen soap ('Smells like clean sheets!' sings the screen), as she washes herself away.

The magnolia. Grandiflora. It was real once, or where did she get the name? How would she ever think of such a thing? Or make up the smell, that flaunting animal smell?

She stands in the kitchen, and the kitchen tells her the time, the kitchen shines like a fresh peach, the kitchen says she looks great today, the kitchen says . . . dose!

She's been overdoing it lately, having too much, overriding the timer on the dose-maid, despite its little squawks of protest and concern. *Do you think that's wise, Suzanne?* It can't go on. She knows that, okay. She knows that. It's just simple chemistry, like he says.

No one ever listens to her stories.

And who should she blame? He is convenient for her. His fame, this house, the comfort, the safety: convenient. She circles him like a dead moon around a planet, a moon that's long ago forgotten why it spins.

But,
But,
But,

How did I come here? She remembers the Old Quarter, low fires burning in the streets, dogs skulking, him hurrying her along, stumbling in her heels, his voice reaching her in bursts, *you can't stay here you can't stay here*

I remember after. My perfect neck turned, pearls in my ears. Snap, my image telegraphed to the gossip screens, his arm heavy over my shoulders like the pelt of an animal.

Sometimes she wishes that she could talk to his girl-friends. His interest in them is limited these days, she's noticed that, but her interest in talking to them: well, she has so many questions! So much she'd like to know.

She was a wondrous doll, once. Shiny hoofs and winsome forelock, a wondrous pony. But now she pulls the cart of herself around the house, broken-winded, dead-eyed, reflected in too many mirrors. He lives inside his enigmatic head, she in hers. She is wallpaper, furniture.

She wakes up on the kitchen table, that gleaming rink, her face pressed and reddened. The clock is choiring softly, urgently, 'Ten, ten, ten.'

And she knows, she just knows, she has been dreaming.

5

James, do you love me? Do you love me?

They always ask him. Her flat out, him with tentative touches, looks, measured speeches delivered at odd times of the day, before breakfast, late at night, when they meet by accident in the long hallways of the house.

'James, you know, when I wasn't much older than you . . .'

'James, one thing you have to understand about . . .'

'James, did you sleep well?'

When he's in his room it's alright. But then he has to come out and he's lost again, sucked into their orbit.

What he likes is to sit in his room, pleasantly, drawing the view from his window. His harness isn't too small, really. Hardly too small at all. It's his first harness, the one they gave him on his fourth birthday. 'Plenty of room to grow,' Aquila had said. These days he tries not to grow at all. He tries to think small and ball-like, to keep his wrists curled tightly in bed, stopping the creep of his cells. He eats scarcely at all. Sometimes she doesn't notice if he puts his shake in the smart waiter half finished. He drinks a lot of tea and that distracts her. Although she is not easily distracted, not from him.

'Fish, fish, fish,' he whispers. They open their long-fringed eyes.

Were they sleeping? Do they sleep?

As soon as he speaks they twine prettily in their bowl, candy-bright, striped and gleaming, so pop-mouthed they look constantly surprised, humming under the water, breaking the surface to sing aloud. He sings with them for a few bars, the highest part of the harmony, and they vibrate their tails, pleased.

They are not real? *She* is not real. She is not.

He holds up his harness and looks at the shape of it, the size.

He holds up his wrists and tries to gauge if they have thickened.

He will do another picture, there is time.

By a series of ingenious manoeuvres, jackknifing, wriggling, he makes it into the harness. He makes his shoulders very small, sparrow-small. He sits still at the desk, tugs once against the handgrips, and waits.

Sparrow. If he closes his eyes he can see it, hopping the length of his sill, possessed of a small purpose. It turns its head and looks at him. The eye dark and cunning. He doesn't move, doesn't breathe. The sparrow shivers its wings contemptuously, puffs its chest, lets out a cry and flies away.

Where?

He was young enough, once, to ask questions. 'Where do the birds come from?'

'What birds?' Suzanne said.

'The birds behind my eyes.'

'You see them?'

'Yes.' He doesn't know what she means. They are there, he sees them.

She looks at him. 'Where did you learn that word, "bird"? What kind of birds? What colour? How many?'

She asks so many questions that he sinks into himself and won't answer. This is how he learns not to ask questions, because all she will do is ask more questions, and he never gets to know where the birds come from, or where they go.

When he makes drawings with birds in them, he hides them afterwards. He has a place for that.

The birch is a quiet tree.

From his window – a floor-length frame of glass – he can see their gentle silver trunks, twisting towards each other, bowing politely.

Sometimes his head surprises him. Like someone is talking in it, not talking to him, but to itself. He likes to listen.

The birch is a quiet tree. It listens.

His hands twitch in the harness.

When you love something, there are a thousand ways to draw it. A thousand thousand ways. You could draw it every day. You could draw it all day. And always something new.

He focuses his love.

His father taught him that. Once very late at night. James was in the hallway, walking in the special way he'd developed so as not to wake Suzanne. The way you did it was to put your foot down very deliberately. You started with the heel and rolled it down slowly slowly slowly. Until it came all the way to the toe and then you stepped. If you did it right she didn't wake. It was hard to do it right. The carpets were so deep they tipped you sideways. You had to concentrate very hard. So hard that sometimes he forgot where he was, and that's when he would begin to hear those slow, calm voices, whispering in his head. *That's what I told you. That's what I told you.*

'James.'

His father was a dark shape at the end of the hall.

'What are you doing?'

'I want a drink.'

'What about the siphon? In your room?'

'It's empty.'

'Oh.'

They faced each other, each rocking a little on their heels.

'I've been meaning to tell you something.'

He waited.

'Very important.'

He waited.

'Your drawings. You're very talented, you know. As

you'd expect. But it's curious, Charity never . . .'

Aquila trailed off, turned his head to the side. His face was hidden. There was a glass in his hand with an inch of clear liquid in it.

James waited, poised on one foot.

'But here's the thing, James: talent, it's not a blind bit of good. Without love. You have to love what you're doing, somehow. The picture you're making. Or the way you're feeling. Or the people you're making it for. Something. That's what makes it, makes it . . .' He gestured vaguely.

'What do you love?' James said.

'What did you say?'

James was silent. The question had escaped him before he had known it.

They stood, listening to the musical hum the house made, the wires, the system. In the day it sounded cheerful, but with all the lights out it was secret, knowing, close in his ear.

'Why would you ask that?'

'I don't know.'

Then Suzanne's door opened and she was there, leaning in the door, one hand going to her lips to light the cigarette.

Aquila said sharply, 'I've told you about that.'

'Yes, I believe you have,' she said, taking a long drag.

'The boy.'

'*The boy,*' she mimicked. 'His name is James.'

'Yes – James.'

'What are you doing up, anyway?' she said, turning on him.

'I was . . . thirsty.'

'Bullshit. I filled your siphon before I put you to bed.'

'I forgot.'

'Really.'

'I was going to the kitchen.'

'You're always *wandering around*.'

'I just wanted a drink.'

'Well, there's a perfectly good one in your bedroom.'

He turned and went down the hall. The low hiss of his parents talking to each other followed him until he closed his door, sealing himself into quiet air.

And that was the end of that.

But he has never forgotten what his father said. He thinks about it. What does he love?

The birch trees, the fish, the reindeer T-shirt, the harness. The harness.

His bed with its pale wood, the fresh green pillow. The deep bath, the way his breath sounds when his ears are below the water. Like it's another person breathing. The smooth expanse of his desk. The feel of the membrane when he peels it.

What does he love?

Suzanne? Aquila?

The way Aquila pours his berries at breakfast, business-like, seeming very interested in the outcome.

The way Suzanne looks when no one's looking: far-off, sometimes smiling.

He puts his hand to his mouth, clenching it, biting the clench.

The harness strains.

Enough.

He sits slackly, exhausted, pulls his hands free. The projector chatters. He stands, tottering a little, the harness hanging loose, and takes the membrane.

It fits in his palm, glowing a little. He waits. Sees the shapes forming under its skin.

Outside his window, the light is clear and pale and golden as honey.

He peels the membrane and crumples the spent skin. The exposed image fits slickly into the end of the projector. There is a low burble and the picture drops, wet, onto the carpet.

He picks it up by the edges and sets it on the desk.

On the damp paper, Suzanne sits beneath a birch tree, her hands full of black-beaked birds. Her face is turned up to the sky. A long shadow falls across her lap.

He waits until the picture dries, the edges curling. Sits and looks at it for a long time. Then rolls it and puts it between his bed and the wall, pushing it down until it disappears.

6

Aquila, the phone breathes.
    Aquila.

'What is it,' he snaps. It's the fourth time today she's called. This time she's framed in red fur, wrapped in it, as if she's killed a crimson animal.

He is engaged in a search for one of his socks.

'Oh, you're getting dressed now?' Antoinette says. 'All dressed up in a suit?'

'No, just, you know . . . dressed.'

'I thought there was a party tonight.'

'How do you know that?'

She looks a little, a very little, discomfited. 'I heard it.'

'I think you have been listening again, Antoinette.' She is a master codebreaker, fast, intuitive; every now and then she likes to crack into their system.

'Alright, there is a party. Family. My daughter's birthday. Okay?'

'That sounds very boring. And your daughter is a bitch, three times, ten times a bitch.'

He sighs, checks underneath the bed. 'You want me to come to the city. Am I right? Have I hit upon it?'

She shrugs, exposing one gleaming shoulder. 'It would be so bad?'

'It's not possible.'

'Why? Why not?'

'This is a special day. For Charity.'

'The party is not until tonight, *chien*. I happen to know this.'

'I have many things to do.'

'There are many hours until tonight.'

He looks at her incendiary mouth, her proud throat, her fur the colour of fresh blood.

'It's true,' he says slowly, and she smiles – with triumph, or perhaps contempt.

He is still a matter of simple chemistry.

'But I can't meet you in the city.'

'Why not?'

'Because I don't want to, sugar. The Meadows, or nothing. That's the deal.'

Her mouth trembles on the edge of invective, then she sits back, arranging herself. 'Certainly, *ami*. The Meadows. Our usual room. I will organise everything.'

He bows. 'You're too good to me, *chérie*.'

'Two o'clock.'

'I may be a little late.'

'No,' she says, letting the fur slip bewitchingly. 'You will not be late.'

The lens goes opaque.

He resumes the search for his sock, a rueful smile lingering at the corner of his mouth.

He wonders if one day he will retire from all of this. Give up his antlers, cease to rut. He's starting to regard young and beautiful women with the calm, appreciative eye of an observer. He's losing his taste for the scalp, the pelt. He wants to watch from afar, mildly, the kind of connoisseur who spits the wine out after tasting. Maybe this will become his foible, his fetish. He'll become the kind of old man who hires young lovers to posture and contort before him. And Antoinette will oblige him even in this. She and her nine young cocks.

He pauses a little to let the self-pity wash through him, warm as bathwater, then shrugs at himself in the mirror.

And still, he can't find the sock. He remembers getting both socks from the thank-you-jeeves just before Antoinette called. Is he going all to pieces?

Aquila.

At first he thinks it's the phone calling to him again, and turns for a moment, confused: but it's Suzanne, standing by his bed with his left sock (a fine-grained argyle) in her hand.

She rarely comes into his room. He can't remember the last time.

'I found this on the carpet. Outside James's room.'

James's room? He hasn't been near James's room. He has been in his own room, talking to Antoinette, since he took the socks from the thank-you-jeeves. Yet here is the sock, left match to his right, same subtle diamond.

'Thank you,' he says guardedly. The most likely explanation is that she's trying to play mind games, has perhaps even sneaked in the room when he was talking to Antoinette.

And taken her small revenge.

She deposits the sock on the bed, and he picks it up. These are the kinds of exchanges they have these days: like two diplomats from enemy countries, negotiating the barter of documents on a bridge.

'Outside James's room,' he says, searching her face for signs of dissimulation.

'Yes. You must have dropped it.'

She's looking him straight in the eye, but that means nothing. She has always had the ability to look him straight in the eye while lying to him. In fact, he can sometimes *tell* that she's lying by her clear, noble gaze.

She indicates his dressing gown, a magnificent affair, a gift from an ambassador, all black silk and embroidered mythical beasts.

'You're getting dressed already?'

'Yes. I have things to do.'

'Going to the city?'

'No.'

'You haven't forgotten, I devoutly hope, your promise to Charity.'

He places his foot lovingly inside the sock, straightening the seams, playing for time.

'You've forgotten.'

'I don't know that I have so much . . . forgotten . . . as . . .'

'As what?'

'Well, I've made a lot of promises to Charity, one way or another . . .'

'Let me give you a hint. Two cups of flour . . .'

'Oh mud gods.'

'Four tablespoons of butter . . .'

'Oh gods of reeking clay.'

'Or in other words, yes.'

'Alright, alright, yes. Did you remind me? Even when you were ordering for the week?'

'Did I make the promise? Besides, these are not things you can *order*. Milk, eggs? I haven't seen them since, since . . .'

'Even so. Simple mercy, Suzanne. Your own safety. Think – Charity turns up. Steps out of lift. Looks around for spectacular handmade cake. Finds nothing but the usual array of elaborate decorations and extravagant gifts. And then. Before her little kitten heel is even across the threshold . . .'

'But I don't have to imagine such a thing. *Thank God*. Because you, as the doting – or should I say dotard – papa who has out of the blue, for no reason, made such a dangerous, *dangerous* promise, will be making so very very sure that when Charity steps out of the lift, she will see the aforementioned, handmade, spectacular triumph of a cake.'

Suzanne is enjoying herself hugely, hand on hip, cobra-swaying.

He takes a shirt from the thank-you-jeeves, his mind racing.

'What will you do?' says Suzanne, with what appears to be innocent curiosity.

'Something. I'll do something.'

'Soon? Will you do the something soon?'

'Soonest. Now.'

'Maybe Antoinette could bring the ingredients with her to the Meadows,' she says serenely, and sits down (as she never does) on his bed.

'So you *were* listening. You did take the sock.'

'Sock? I wasn't listening, no. I don't have to. You're going somewhere. Where do you ever go? To meet her. At the Meadows, these days. Because you don't like to go to the city anymore. Right? So will you call up this latest goddess of yours and beg at her feet for the favour of some butter, a little vanilla?'

She has a point. She has a solid, well-formed point.

'Uh, would you like to be here? While I do that?'

'Good question. Would I? I would, kind of. I would like to see her face when you ask. And yet . . .' Suzanne shrugs, turns, and trails out of the room, on her way out tapping his Übermensch Award so it falls with a heavy thunk onto the carpet.

Wearily, he summons Antoinette.

—

All the way down in the lift, he rails against himself.

He remembers now the day he made Charity the promise. One of their awkward lunches, perched around the long dining table, everything carefully polished. Charity had brought up her birthday and he and Suzanne had sneaked glances at each other, hoping it would be one of the wonderful, blessed birthdays when she'd decide to stay in the city and celebrate with her friends (the kind of friends she always assembles around herself, drawn by her fame and wealth and the hard, bright light of her, quickly gone), but it was obviously one of the other kinds. The kind where she's decided that she wants to 'be with the family'. And they had warbled 'Of course, of course, how lovely, dinner?' And she'd said yes, dinner, and her mouth had already been curling with disappointment, and it is his task, his holy mission, to at all times keep that from happening, and so he'd cast around desperately and come up with (curse his brain, curse the particular dumb, rogue synapse responsible) the idea of the cake.

The lift stops and he punches the button, hard. The doors open and he steps into the dim blue light of the catazoom.

If he could just order it from the smart waiter, like a normal person. But she will know, she will test its texture and her face will twist with anger.

In his pocket is the recipe he's cadged from Arkhive. He takes it out and examines it as he fits his feet onto the walkway and punches (hard) the destination button.

'Cream' butter and sugar? 'Cream' them? Does this mean to add cream? God knows how he will afford that; the butter and milk alone are going to clean him out. Dairy is always the most expensive. They say it's the hardest to replicate, something to do with the way the molecules separate. Yet (he scans quickly) there is nothing about cream in the list of ingredients. There were no notes with the recipe; in fact, Arkhive told him, in its parched, didactic voice, that he was lucky to get so much.

Arkhive irks him. The idea is that it mimics the voice of a librarian, but he's too used to his melodious house. He resents its tone.

'Beat' the egg? Does this mean to smash it? Surely not.

Since he made the new sculpture, whenever he thinks of the house, that kindly haven, an unease twists his gut and stirs his cock and hackles, as if the thing crouched under its sheet was a seed in him, growing black roots through his veins, wires it can tug.

Beat the egg?

Thank God for Antoinette, who had actually been surprisingly accommodating about the whole thing, quite the good sport, promised to run straight out to the Old Quarter and make it to the Meadows by the time agreed.

'You won't be late?' he'd asked, trying not to sound anxious.

'Of course not,' she'd cooed. 'See you, *ange*.' And she'd blown him a kiss.

In his pocket, his screen emits a small, mellifluous cry. He has even less time than he thought. Even though the marker lights (a sprightly blue that always makes him a bit nauseous) are moving by so fast they are streaks at the corners of his eyes, he wills the walkway faster.

How quickly can he satisfy Antoinette? He must be nicer than usual. He owes her, and she knows it. He must be charming. He has never really had to be charming before. She came after him, from the first moment. She has chased, seduced, hounded.

The lights slow from streaks to round, cold moons; a crisp voice says 'The Meadows'. He unlatches his feet and forearms from the walkway and steps into the lift.

The foyer of the Meadows is a vast expanse of carpet, expensively simulating an actual meadow, sprigged with buttercups and dandelions that blow their silver clocks softly into the air with the breeze of his passage.

At reception, he asks a garlanded nymph for the keys to his usual room. She ('Certainly, Aquila') hands him the key (in the shape of a shepherd's crook – sometimes this place is too arch for words) and then he is in another lift, gazing into its many mirrors at the sour look on his face.

The Arcadia Suite, his regular room, is a full-blown penthouse with a view that reaches almost to the city: he can see the faint glitter of it at the edge of the horizon, the curvature of the dome. The room is done up like an alpine glade. The bed is nestled into a grove of gingerbread-ish mountains that reach to the high ceiling. The carpet is thick with violets; their skilfully replicated scent gives the room a cloying smell he's never liked. He should perhaps ask for another room next time. The Prairie Suite, maybe. Just rolling, silken grass.

He takes off his clothes, grimaces at himself in the mirror, puts on one of the snowy robes hanging in the snowy bathroom, falls onto the ice-blue satin sheets, and tries to get himself in the mood, as they say, for love.

Not long afterwards, Antoinette sails through the door, glances at him where he lies on the bed, fumbling inside his robe, and says contemptuously, 'Did you miss me, then, p'tit?'

'Of course,' he says, keeping his hand on his cock, in order to avoid the appearance of having been surprised. She's looking, as usual, a knockout in a long white fur that she insouciantly shucks to reveal her improbable body, clad only in a vestigial playsuit and collar that look as if they're made of white, glowing shell. Against her plum-dark skin the effect is dizzying.

'Did you wear that to the Old Quarter?'

She shrugs. 'Yes, why not? There was no risk. I had outriders with me, three of them.'

'Not nine?'

She laughs, pleased. 'You remember, hmmm? I think you remember me with the nine young beautiful men. You think about it.'

'Of course,' he says, showing her the erection he has almost managed.

She smiles in a way he can't quite decipher and wanders around the suite, showing off the spectacular spectacle she is, idly straightening a paperweight with a turreted castle inside it, taking and biting a snow pear from an immense bowl.

'Come here,' he commands, trying his best not to

sneak a look at the time, via the ludicrous cuckoo clock on the wall. But she keeps meandering around the room, and he doesn't like the look of that smile.

'You would like to have me, then?'

'Sure,' he says, then, as an afterthought, 'baby.'

'You really would?'

'Who wouldn't? Look at you.'

'Exactly!' she flashes. 'Who wouldn't? Everyone wants to, everyone. I could have five men before I was even out of my building. The doormen want me, the lift boy, the concierge, I get into a hansom and the driver's eyes are on me in the mirror.'

'I'm not surprised,' he says evenly.

'And yet you would rather cower in your house, where everything is nice and safe and the world doesn't come, where everything calls you sir, than be a man and come to me. You would rather have breakfast with your dead-eyed hag of a wife than take me to bed. *Hein?*'

'Antoinette' – this is doing absolutely nothing for his hard-on, incidentally – 'here I am. I'm here. Aren't I? So why don't you come on over here and, you know . . .?'

'Yes. You are here. Not in the city, but *here*. So every now and then, when you decide that I have been very good and deserve you, you do not come to the city, oh no, you do not take me to the cloud bars and to the unveilings and the flash theatres and to eat at Phalanx, no, you make me come here to you, to your room, like something you have bought!'

'Antoinette. You're screaming. Did you know that? Listen, if it's to be seen with me you want, what's the point? Everyone knows that you're my, my . . .'

'Your *what*?'

Semantics. Bad area.

He takes a risk. 'Suzanne calls you my goddess.'

She stops mid-stride, the mauled pear in her hand. 'Your wife talks about me?'

'Not usually. Not often. Today.'

'Was she angry? Did *she* scream?'

Oh, how her eyes glow, how she relishes this. 'She was angry, I think she was very angry, but she didn't scream, no.'

'Ha. Your wife calls me your goddess.'

She sits on the edge of the bed and takes a triumphant piece out of the pear with her excellent teeth. The fruit collapses, hissing, and she chews boisterously, looking him over.

'Next time, you will come to the city.'

'Yes.'

'We will go out.'

'Alright. Okay.'

After all, he does get it, what she wants. It's not enough that everyone knows she's captured him: she wants to drag him around the city, she wants them to see the fine time she's having. He felt the same, once, with his mezzanine tables, far above the proles, the cynosure of all eyes, drunk on it. It wouldn't hurt him. To take her out a little, maybe once or twice.

'Alright, cherry blossom. Next time, I'll come to the city. You'll get all dressed up, I'll buy you something new to wear, something marvellous, expensive. And we'll go to Phalanx, or the New Tourettes.'

'Both.' She extends a long, insolent leg, presents him with her foot. As he mouths at it, he turns his head slyly to the cuckoo clock.

Oh Götterdämmerung. Oh death of all the gods.

'So, baby, did you, ah –'

She kicks him, lightly, on the jaw.

'Did I save your ass? Yes. The ingredients are in my bag. We'll talk about it' – she pushes her foot at his mouth – 'later.'

'I should pay you. Those things are expensive.'

'I charged them to your card.'

With one of those ninja gymnast moves that always make him flinch slightly, she snatches back her foot and lands on her knees, straddling him.

'So I think you would be very grateful. *Non?*'

'You will never know how much.'

'You are mistaken. I will know exactly how much. Because you will show me, now.'

'Well, the thing is, *mignon* . . .'

'There is no thing. Proceed.'

He looks feverishly at the clock, which, as if in response, spits out an impudent cuckoo that bows, calls the hour smugly and closes its door with a snap.

Antoinette glowers.

'If we hurry . . . if we're very quick . . . but *mon chou*, Charity . . .'

'Very quick! When were you ever anything else!'

She retrieves herself and throws the wet remains of the pear into the mirror, which trembles for a moment, then continues to reflect, placidly, her rage.

She upturns the fruit bowl, sending perfect strawberries and quinces and Golden Delicious apples scudding into the corners.

'So, not only am I your paid whore, I am also your shopgirl, your errand girl, is this it?'

'No, no, not whore. Goddess, remember? *Ange*, please . . .'

'*Espèce d'ordure!*' She flings the fur around her and storms to the door, snatching up a big white fur tote on the way out.

'Antoinette! Please, the ingredients, please!'

'Oh yes,' she turns, 'I was forgetting, *non*?' And she takes, one by one, the priceless, precious ingredients, and throws them at him: the butter hits him in the jaw, the sack of flour in the eye (bursting), the cachous rain around him. He recovers and rushes her, seizing her wrists as she reaches for the eggs: they struggle, she with all the strength of her furious youth, he with sheer, panicked desperation. After she's clawed at him a little, spat in his face and kneed his balls, she lets go, wheels in a cloud of fur and kicks her way out of the room, taking a chunk out of the woodwork.

He kneels, sobbing for breath, holding an egg in each hand.

The phone calls his name. A cool voice from reception, asking if he would like a maid to 'set the room to rights'.

'After,' he wheezes.

He curls up on the carpet, assessing all the different

pains that are ricocheting through him. The balls are the worst, the pain there flooding his loins like the dark flipside of orgasm, settling at his waist. That distracts him for a moment from the tenderness of the fast-swelling jaw, the throbbing eye, the raked cheek.

He is too old for girls like her. They are a young man's game.

The cuckoo, incredibly, appears again, nodding with each little call, the half hour this time, same smartly closed gaily painted little door.

He would like to crush it in his fist.

He closes his eyes and pretends for one beautiful, beautiful moment that he's in the bath, about to have a long refreshing look at *Hive*, then battles onto all fours. The eggs, which he's placed tenderly in the plush depths of a violet patch, seem to be unharmed. Laboriously, he picks up every cachou. He scrapes the carpet with his fingernails until he salvages most of the flour. The butter, the sugar is intact. The milk bottle, miraculously, is whole. He has a short but potent ordeal that involves a lot of groaning and ends with him crawling backwards from under the bed, bottles of vanilla and cochineal gripped doggedly in his fists.

'Piece of cake,' he says under his breath, and snickers.

Clothes. He buffets his way into them, figuring the quicker the better. The socks are the worst. After he's dressed he sits on the bed, contemplates a gentle sob, thinks better of it and gathers the ingredients in one of the complimentary totes.

In the lift's mirrors he already looks beaten up.

He was hoping that he would be able to get out of the place before the damage was visible, but no such luck. He wanders into reception to pay his bill, attempting *sangfroid*, and watches them trying to avoid looking at his face.

He wonders what rumours will spread over the city tomorrow about him and Antoinette and what they get up to in bed.

He looked as if he'd gone three rounds with his daughter . . . is that why he likes it that way? My dear . . .

What matter, he has the ingredients. He places the tote with finicking care on the package rack of the walkway, keeping a hand on it, then pushes the destination button and closes his eyes.

Take me home.

7

Suzanne steps back from the teetering mountain of presents, examining the effect.

When she puts both hands on her waist, she feels the thickening there. Compared to the way it used to be, whip-supple, in her youth. She thinks, she knows. So her waist has thickened. That's a sign of a body that has carried babies. Isn't it? She has searched herself carefully. There are no scars, true. There are signs of wear, stretch, but this could just be age, and besides, her creams eradicate them so quickly she can't be sure of the exact pattern.

Charity with her back to the door. Remember? Her narrow child's back, her blonde head bent over the baby, telling him something she can't hear.

'James,' she calls sharply.

Nothing.

She backs away, step by step, from the quivering

presents and swishes down the hall. He never comes when she calls, never. Although if she goes down there and opens the door, he will do what he does now, which is to stop whatever he's doing and stand dutifully in front of her, his hands at his sides.

'What are you doing?'

'Nothing.'

'How can you be doing nothing?'

'I don't know. I just was. I was looking.'

'At what?'

He glances behind him, as if casting around for an idea.

'Out of the window.'

'What did you see?'

'Nothing.'

'That doesn't make any sense.'

'I wasn't trying to make sense. I was just looking.'

'At nothing.'

'Yes. Sometimes I want to do that. Sometimes *you* do that.'

He seems angry, for some reason, today. Sometimes he gets like this. Grey, fretful. His skin a little grey. He doesn't look so well, lately. He looks like an old man.

'Well,' she says, humouring him, 'perhaps I do. Yes, perhaps I do. Anyway, what about tonight? Decided what you're going to wear?'

'Not yet, no. I have to look in the thank-you-jeeves.'

'Well, for God's sake, don't leave it too late,' she says in alarm. 'She'll be here at five.'

'I forgot to tell you,' he says. 'She rang.'

'*What?*'

'Yeah, she rang. A little while ago, while you were lying down.'

'Why didn't you call me?'

'She didn't want me to.'

'Well? What did she want?'

'She wanted to tell you that she'd be a little late. And that she's bringing her new boyfriend.'

'Her what? Her *what*?'

James says nothing.

'Perfect. This just gets better. Your father goes missing, the ordering's already done, and now . . .'

'She said not to worry about dinner and things. She said he doesn't eat much.'

'Really? Huh. He can't be a bounter, then. And were you going to tell me about this, sometime?'

'I was going to. But then you were lying down. And then I forgot.'

'What with all the staring out the window at nothing.'

'I guess.'

She gives up. Throwing her hands in the air, sighing gustily, she gives up. They can't be hers. It's not possible that your children could be so little on your side.

There is no one on her side, no one.

She thinks she's going to cry, but she swallows hard and stares at the colour of the sky – a soft pearl – until the moment passes.

'Okay,' she says, sounding a bit throaty. 'Thanks for telling me.'

'No problem,' he says, eyeing her strangely.

'Let me know when you're dressed? I want to check you over.'

'Okay.'

His door closes with its almost inaudible click. It seems like every time she leaves his room she's suffered some defeat she doesn't even properly understand. It wears her out.

Boyfriend?

Charity has a boyfriend?

Oh, she's had them before, of course. Some of them have even lasted longer than a week. So she hears, so she sees, when she bothers to browse her screen. Charity parading around with some bright new thing on her arm. Just like her father.

But a 'boyfriend' . . .

The word is so unlike her. As is the bringing to dinner.

Anyway (*deep breath, deep breath*), she has no time for this. She has to do her ikebana.

She takes a quick look at the dining room to see how the decorations are getting on. The table is already glimmering with a faint blue stain. The decorations she chose – intricate shapes akin to shells and flowers, but heavier, more grandiose – are multiplying from alkaloid crystals in the corners of the room, along the architraves and in the centre of the table. Unfolding themselves, growing quietly and secretly.

In the kitchen, the smart waiter lies open, spilling flowers and twigs. She's chosen delphiniums, blue irises, pussy willow twigs: calming blues, the colours that sat behind certain clouds on certain still, hot days, in the old days. There is her china bowl, cream, with spidery cracks in the glaze.

The dying art of ikebana. She likes the simple pitting of a few sharp elements against themselves. The simplicity of the bowls. The symbolic meanings of the flowers, now almost lost.

She closes her eyes and begins.

This, at least, is something she remembers. Right? The way she learnt ikebana. Coming home from the Click Barn, carrying about eight bags of shopping, in that street she lived in when she first came to the city, a long street of low windows, whole fish lying on slabs, flies at their mouths. She had put down the shopping bags to rest her aching arms. She was wearing scuffed purple boots with pansies stitched into them and the Indian cobbler offered to fix them, to sew the leather that was curling away from the toes.

'Look,' he said. 'Miss, you are about to lose a flower.'

'I was deflowered long ago,' she said, half weary, half provocative.

She opens her eyes, startled, to find the kitchen, her kitchen, humming cheerfully to itself, glinting. Does she remember this? Or is it a film she's seen? What street was that? What is a cobbler? But she can see his scarred face, his guarded smile, and he takes her foot in his hand.

Real cherry blossom. He sold real cherry blossom for fifteen bucks a branch. They have never got that polleny smell right, in the replication. It's too sweet, what they've done. She never buys it.

She closes her eyes again. Assembles the pebbles. Smooth and deliberate in her hands. Places the three twigs, with their silver-furred buds. Three of them: heaven, earth and man. A scalene triangle.

Her hands smooth the bowl. Cracked, that means beauty. Imperfection is perfection.

Her breathing slows and steadies. Now she can open her eyes. The twigs are placed just right, perfect first time. The long heaven twig pointing plaintively at the ceiling.

'No heaven here,' she tells it.

The blue flowers: two irises, one delphinium. Again she closes her eyes.

'Playing with your sticks again?'

She opens her eyes, furious.

'Where in the hell have you been?' Then she takes in his appearance: his, it would seem, recently beaten state.

'You know where I've been.'

'Yes, but, how –'

'I don't actually want to talk about it.'

He hauls a Meadows tote onto the island bench.

'The ingredients.'

'Thank the *goddess* for that.'

'Indeed. Now I just have to work out how to make this thing.'

'And make up a story to explain,' she gestures at his roughed-up-ness, 'this . . .'

'Yes, "this". So, how did it happen? Any ideas?'

'How *did* it happen?'

'That's not important. We have to think of something.'

'*We* have to think of something?'

The pussy willow twig trembles, and drops a bud.

'Alright, *I* do. But you could help, couldn't you? Could you at least do that?'

'At least?'

'Yes, at least. I've been out there, on the outside, getting all this together, at great personal expense I may add, while you stay here in comfort, messing about with pebbles –'

'Why do you always refer to it as if it's some kind of kindergarten project?' Suzanne cups her hands around the bowl, feeling the pattern of its cracks.

'Can we get back to the matter at hand?'

'You'll be pleased to hear that she's going to be a little late.'

'Good. How late?'

'I'm not sure. James talked to her. He said that she'll be bringing – her boyfriend.'

'Really? Boyfriend? Good. Perhaps she'll be calmer if she's got someone in tow.'

He scrabbles together her ikebana things and dumps them on a side bench. For a moment she considers wandering off to her room and letting him fend for himself, but that would not, in the end, be smart.

'What kind of cake is it?'

'A cake, I don't know what kind. What does it say, it says,' he scrabbles in his pocket, 'marble cake.'

'Sounds – hmmm. Kind of undelicious.'

'That was the first one Arkhive gave me. I didn't have time to mess around.'

'It says bowls. Hot water.'

They fossick madly in cupboards, call to the smart waiter.

'It doesn't have bowls that big.'

'Ask it for the salad one. Quickly!'

'"Sift"?'

'It must mean through your fingers.'

'Alright. But what does "cream" mean?'

'Is there cream?'

'No.'

'There must be a mistake somewhere. This is doomed.'

'I think,' he holds the bridge of his nose with one hand, kneads the air with the other, 'I think you do something with a fork.'

'A fork. We have one of those.'

He hovers over the bowl with it, looking so much like one of his 'great artist' photos that Suzanne cracks up laughing. She can't help it.

'Do you think you should go get your harness?'

'Oh, *shut up*.'

'What have you been making, anyway? What have you got down there in your studio? It's taking you long enough.'

He pours the sugar over the fork, watching it slither into the bowl. 'I don't really want to talk about it.'

'Why not?'

'It's not; it's not . . .'

'What?'

'Like the others. I don't know what to say about it.'

'Oh. Anyway – I don't think that can be right,' she says, looking dubiously at the lumpy, grainy mess rising out of the bowl.

'It'll be fine.' He beats at it with the whole strength of his arm.

'Is it bigger?'

'What?'

'The sculpture. How is it different? Bigger? More figurative? You have maybe a Venus or a Daphne down there?'

'Don't be ridiculous. What else has to go in?'

'This – it says "drops".'

'Well, drop it in.'

He slugs the dark liquid at the mixture.

'Wait – it says you have to separate the eggs. What does that mean, one at a time? Hang on, milk . . . what the hell is cochineal?'

'This.'

'Is there another salad bowl?'

'I don't think so.'

In the end they panic and throw everything in and mix it together frantically, then throw it in the smart waiter and turn the reheat function up as far as it will go.

'Doomed,' says Suzanne.

'Let's worry about that later. I have to get dressed. Is the dining room . . .?'

'Yes, it's fine. It's all growing, it's fine.'

'Look – thanks,' he says.

She nods. 'While you're getting dressed, think of a story for the face.'

'Rough day in the pastry quarter?' He smiles crookedly and heads for his bedroom.

The kitchen fills with the smell of burning. She sighs and picks up an iris, which is cracked in the middle, the head dangling.

8

In the end, of course, they wait for Charity.

The dining room is a triumph, the table a deep, glowing blue, the walls blooming with luscious reds, a fantastical centrepiece that resembles crimson orchids crossed with skyscrapers. They are dressed in sleek harmony, Suzanne in a floor-length harebell satin gown, he in a dinner suit with burgundy satin detailing, James in a button-cute number that makes him look something like a tiny harlequin. The house smells subtly of wine, of flowers. They are standing in front of the lift, not because they have planned to, but because they have all drifted there, like iron filings dragged by a magnet. Suzanne, despite his complaints, is smoking. He is not quite wringing his hands.

Five, five, chortle the clocks.

They are ready. They are tight and shiny as bubbles, ready to pop.

And they wait.

Because Charity is always late. Except when she is suddenly, disastrously early.

'Perhaps you should take another look at the cake,' says Suzanne, mostly managing to conceal her snigger.

'Can we not talk about the cake?'

'No, really. All things considered, it turned out pretty well. I mean, it's a cake, fairly much immediately identifiable as a cake. It has a cake-like form. Even smells like cake. A burnt one.'

'Do you have to?'

'No, not have to. It's just that it's kinda fun. Passes the time.' She lights another cigarette from the butt of the last.

'For pity's sake, Suzanne. Must you?'

'No, not must. It's just that it's kinda –'

'Alright. *Alright*.'

'It is? Oh, thank you so much.' She holds the heavy crystal ashtray in one hand, ashing in it with the other.

'You know that it's bad for James,' he says. 'Could weaken his breathing.'

'Sorry,' Suzanne tells James, taking another long drag. 'It's okay.'

'Don't tell her that,' snaps Aquila.

'You just said yourself it was alright,' she snaps back.

'Do you have to do this? We're all on edge.'

'Except for James,' she says, indicating the boy, who is standing with his eyes closed, breathing quietly.

'You think?'

'You're not on edge, are you? James?'

'No,' he says, his eyes still closed.

'You look pretty suave, darling.'

'Thanks.'

'Like a little . . . jester.'

'Thanks.'

'Shall we have a drink?' Suzanne asks. 'Shall we have a – you know – aperitif?'

'A what?'

'Perhaps some, uh, Pernod.'

'What a strange idea.'

'I feel like one. I feel like taking something.'

'Pernod? Where would you get such a thing?'

'There's some in the kitchen. I've had it for ages. I've been saving it.'

She sashays off into the kitchen. He finds himself watching her idly, through the doorway. She appears to be nude under the satin dress. What is she dressing like that for? Certainly not for him. Who, then? The boyfriend?

She has a freshly ruffled, daisy-ish look. Awake. Interested.

'You're looking forward to this. Aren't you?' he says as she offers him a glass. The Pernod seems poisonous, milky.

'You must be joking.'

'It's like you get some kind of kick out of it.'

'What kind of kick is that? Head? Guts?'

'You seem very pleased with yourself, is all I'm saying.'

'I don't know what you're accusing me of.'

'Nothing. I'm just noticing.'

'How perfectly uxorious. But why, all of a sudden?'

'Because you're acting strange. Exhilarated. Lit up. Like you're looking forward to Charity's arrival.'

'I'm enjoying my drink. My dress. It feels nice.' She rubs the satin over her hip.

'You know, sometimes I think you should have been the bouncer.'

'Why on earth?'

'Because I think you enjoy a fight.'

'You're the one needling me. I'm just having a Pernod. I think it's you who enjoys a fight. You're the one with the black eye, after all.'

'James,' he says pointedly, 'there are some bowls of roasted pine nuts in the kitchen, on the bench. Could you grab them?'

'Okay,' says James, trailing off in his harlequin's suit. *'Do you mind?'* he hisses at Suzanne, who shrugs.

He fingers the edge of a swollen lip.

'What are you going to tell her, by the way?'

'That I fell?'

'Don't be absurd. She of all people knows how to tell what kind of bruises you get from falling and what kind you get from a fight.'

He considers. 'I'll tell her it happened in the city. Crazed fan. That's it, crazed fan.'

'Nice. With the added advantage of being sort of true.'

James comes back into the room with a bowl in each hand. He gives one bowl to Aquila, one to Suzanne.

'Thank you, apple,' she says.

'No problem.'

'Half past . . . five!' enthuse the clocks.

'Of course, she did *say* she would be late.'

'She just didn't say *how* late.'

'A "bit". Wasn't that it? James?'

The boy looks at his feet. 'I think so. I can't remember.'

'Well, never mind,' Aquila says. 'She'll be here soon enough. Should we sit down?'

'What a wonderful idea,' says Suzanne, plunging a fresh cigarette into the long flame of her lighter.

'Where did you learn that filthy habit?'

Suzanne looks at him in amazement. 'From you.'

'Nonsense.'

'Are you serious? You used to smoke. Prolifically. I took it up after I met you. You made me nervous, in those days.'

'Don't be ridiculous.'

'Which part?'

'I don't smoke. I've never smoked.'

She shakes her head, bemused. 'Why don't we remember the same things?'

'Don't we? We do.'

'No, you used to smoke. I can see you, at the Mare's Tail. With a cheroot.'

'Someone else.'

'There was no one else.'

'How romantic,' he says acidly.

'In those days,' she says with careful emphasis.

He gulps the rest of his Pernod. 'This is disgusting.

Like drinking licorice.'

'I find it rather nice.'

'Have you opened the wine?'

'Ages ago.'

'Then everything's ready.'

'Ages ago.'

'Yes.' They sit on the low flat cream couch, in a row.

'Are you going to show her your new piece?'

He feels a shudder run through him, like an aftershock of the jolts his body had endured as he'd created the deep scores, the deep grains of that work. He's not ready to show it to anyone.

'Can you do me a favour? Don't mention it.'

'That's not like you. You love showing off new work.'

'Not this one, not yet.'

James looks at him too, sidelong.

'Is it in the basement?' he whispers.

'Yes, of course.'

'I thought so.' His son examines the carpet.

Suzanne suggests that they play a game. To pass the time, she says, while they are waiting.

'Really? You feel like playing a game?' he says. 'Charades? What?'

'How about this. You tell me what I was wearing when we first met.'

He waits a beat, then says, 'How about we play something that James can play?'

'James, do you want to hear what I was wearing when Aquila and I first met?'

James hesitates. 'Yes.'

'You see?'

'Suzanne, I don't remember.'

'I thought as much.'

'Do you?'

'I do. I think I do.' She sighs and rests her chin in her hand, gazing into nothing. 'Do you remember my purple boots, with the flowers? That street, with the windows full of dead fish? Do you remember this stuff?'

He shakes his head slightly. 'Can we concentrate on the matter at hand? Charity will be here any minute.'

'Where did we live, when we lived in the city?'

'She'll be here,' he says, walking into the kitchen with his empty glass, 'any minute.'

9

Charity fits Edward into the walkway, then wraps herself tightly around him and punches the destination button.

'It's dangerous,' he murmurs into her ear as they speed up.

'Yes.'

She opens his mouth with her tongue. The wind of their passage howls, flattening her against him. It never ceases to pique her, the sharp feel of his teeth. She licks them.

'You like risks,' he says.

'I like you.'

Rushing through the dark tunnel, the cold lights streaking by like comets, they kiss. His impossible strength is held by the restraints of the walkway. She writhes against him. Fingers his collar.

'Will they like me? Your parents?'

'Of course.'

'It may be a shock to them.'

'I don't care.'

She closes her eyes against the blue wind. His throat, in its stiff linen shirt, smells of her.

'You look magnificent,' she tells him.

'I wanted to look – elegant. For your birthday.'

He says things like this. Small, touching things, things no one has ever said to her before.

The walkway groans, slowing. She arches against him a last time and steps away so he can free himself. The lift is already waiting.

Halfway up, she presses the stop button. The lift shudders to a halt and hangs between floors, rocking a little.

'What are you doing?'

She is looking at them in the mirror, taking an endless picture of them in her mind, stopping time to look at how perfect they are. She tall and strong and golden, honed to an improbable edge, he a hulking darkness, sleek head jutting forward to stare at their reflection, vast arms around her.

She turns to him urgently and pulls at his buttons.

'What are you doing?'

'You know what I'm doing.'

'But they know we're here. They sent the lift.'

'They'll wait.'

'This is not a good start,' he says.

'I don't care about that,' she says, and puts him in her.

As they fuck, her heels scoring the metal walls, she

looks over his shoulder and over her own to the infinite number of them, achieving this perfection. Stopping time.

After, they stand together before the mirror, smoothing themselves down. She adjusts the complicated cut of her dress, delivered that morning by the designer, and helps Edward restore the immaculate set of his tie.

'Do I look wonderful?' she asks him, spinning on the spot.

'Oh yes. Oh yes, Charity.'

'Good. You look wonderful too.' She kisses him on the nose and slaps the button; the lift sighs and resumes its ascent.

She squeezes his hand.

'I really want you to meet my little brother. James. He's only eight. He's an artist, though, I can already tell. A better one than my father.'

'Will I like your father?'

She shrugs one shoulder.

The lift doors slide back and there they are, framed by the calm, reasonable greens of the house, its deep amnesia creams, its blond woods from nowhere, its views shut off by night so that it reflects only itself.

'Charity,' says Aquila, stepping forward. 'Happy birthday, pet lamb.'

The lift door opens fully and they all see Edward.

There is a hushed, poised moment of stillness.

'I brought you something,' she says. 'This is Edward. We're very happy.'

Aquila, she notes with satisfaction, is glue-pale,

looks sick with shock. And, on second glance, someone has beaten him up.

Now this is what she calls a birthday.

Suzanne is the first to recover.

'Happy birthday, Charity.' She stalks over in her tottery heels and leans in to kiss at her daughter's cheek.

'Thank you. The house looks wonderful. Look at all the trouble you've been to.' Charity dumps her bag on the carpet and saunters to the door of the dining room, taking in the pile of presents, the heavy bloomings at the corners of the ceiling. 'Look, Edward. Aren't they sweet to me?'

Edward comes obediently to her side.

She indicates each of them in turn. 'This is my father, Aquila. My mother, Suzanne. And my little brother, *the artist*, James.'

Edward bows a little as she says the names. James moves to stand behind Suzanne.

'James, I have a present for you.'

'But it's *your* birthday,' he says warily.

She sings with laughter. 'Funny boy. I always bring you a present. Remember? We'll have it in a minute. Well . . .' looking around her, 'I think I would like a drink now. Edward?'

Suzanne lurches guiltily. 'I'll get it. We were having Pernod. Would you like to try some?'

'I wouldn't,' says Aquila. At the first attempt, his voice fails, is little better than a growl; he clears his throat and tries again. 'I wouldn't advise it. It's kind of disgusting.'

Suzanne looks crestfallen. Or stunned, one of the two.

'I think I will try it. One for Edward, too,' Charity says. Suzanne veers towards the kitchen.

'Come here, James,' commands Charity. He looks around at Aquila, who nods: he trails over to her. She leans down and crushes him in her arms. He gasps.

'Little man. Look at you. Look at him,' she croons to Edward. 'Isn't he adorable?'

'Hello, James,' says Edward. He takes Charity's arm gently, loosening her grip on James, who stares up at him. 'I like your outfit,' Edward says.

'Thank you.'

'It's cute,' says Charity. 'Little cutie.'

'You smell nice,' whispers James.

She laughs and lets him go.

'Sure I do. It's my own perfume.' She holds her wrist under her nose, savouring. 'Bounter.'

'They called it Bounter?' Suzanne is watching from the doorway.

'Why not? It's what I am. It's why I have a perfume in the first place. They did think about calling it Bounty Hunter. They liked the heritage feel. But I said it was Bounter or nothing. Here. Smell.' She thrusts her wrist out at Suzanne, who approaches with caution, sniffs and retreats a few paces.

'I think they've really got you there. It's . . . you can't miss it.'

'You like it, then,' she mocks. Aquila still hasn't recovered, is sitting on the cream couch with his head fairly much in his hands.

'It's very pretty,' says Suzanne. She hands Charity a glass and turns to Edward. Charity watches the exchange closely: Suzanne lets go of the glass only at the last moment, when she's sure that Edward is able to hold it.

'I've had this Pernod for years,' she says to Charity. 'I can't even remember now where I got it from.'

Charity sniffs, grimaces. 'It smells like my muscle rub.'

'It's an acquired taste.'

'I doubt it.'

'It's supposed to stimulate the appetite.'

'I doubt that too.'

'Give it to me, then,' says Suzanne. 'I'll drink it. You can have something else.'

'I warned you,' says Aquila, in his death's-head voice, from the couch.

Charity frowns, takes a slug of the Pernod and hands it to Suzanne, who drains it.

'Edward? How do you like it?' says Suzanne.

Edward sips, considers.

'Licorice,' he says.

'Yes. Aniseed.'

'What's that?' says Charity.

'A plant. A herb. Do you like it, Edward?'

'I rather do. I think I'll keep it, please. I've never had anything quite like it.'

'By all means, keep it, Edward. In fact, you know what. I'll get us some more.' With a bright glance around the room, Suzanne takes her empty glass into the kitchen.

'My mother likes to drink at parties,' Charity tells Edward.

'Most people do.'

'How about you, Aquila?' she calls to him. 'Won't you be having a drink? Going to tough it out sober?'

'I don't think so, angelfish,' he says. 'I think your mother will bring me something.'

'Always the right doses, at the right moments, in this house, right?'

They stare at each other for a long time.

'You're looking well,' he says.

'I always look well.'

'You look particularly well.'

'I always look particularly well,' says Charity, settling her dress on her hips. 'You, on the other hand . . .'

'Yes, it's not a good day. Wasn't. Wasn't a good day. Now you've arrived, of course –'

'You must tell me all about it. I'd like to hear *all* the details. But let's save it for dinner.'

'I'm not sure it's ideal dinner conversation.'

'I think you're wrong there. Edward? What do you think? I think there's a fascinating story behind, for instance, that class-four cat-rake on his left cheekbone. Wouldn't you like to hear it?'

Edward says, 'You look like you hurt, Aquila. Have you taken something for the pain?'

'Superfluous question,' she scoffs.

'As a matter of fact, I haven't,' he says, staring her down. 'Too much to do, petal-pie.'

She sniffs the air. 'Is that – can that be –'

'I knew you'd remember. Yes,' his smile jubilant, a little mad, 'it's your cake.'

Suzanne sails into the room, a tray of drinks held at shoulder level.

'Edward. More Pernod.'

'I'm afraid I haven't finished this one.'

'That's why God gave you two hands, sweetie.'

Aquila's eyes dart to Edward's hand as he amiably takes the second glass.

'Charity, vodka, straight up.'

'I'm in training.'

'Come on, honey. It's your birthday. We won't tell Coach. Aquila? Vodka? Nice straight-up vodka?'

'Do you know, I think I will.'

'I thought you would.'

'I don't have a drink,' says James, with quiet dignity.

They all laugh uproariously.

'I'm sorry, bluebird. What would you like? Iced tea?'

He nods, and Suzanne wheels back to the kitchen.

'What did she call him?' Charity asks.

'Bluebird,' says Edward.

'How's the run-up to the season going?' says Aquila. He has both elbows on his knees now, seems more balanced.

'Hard. As usual. It gets harder every year.'

'They got good pharmas for you?'

'The best. Of course. Doesn't help, though. Still hell.'

'You don't you get used to it?'

'No.'

Always Charity manages to imply that there is no work as hard as her work, certainly not art; which is, Aquila supposes, true. Although at times, like this last time, for instance, like the sculpture, it can feel very like a struggle to the death.

A silence. Edward sips his drink, holding it up to look at the colour against the light.

'I don't know how you can drink that awful stuff,' Charity says.

'That's quite a dress you have on,' says Aquila.

'Sara Possible.' She performs an abbreviated parade that ends a couple of inches from his nose, whirls, and retreats to stand by Edward.

'Impressive.'

'Do you recognise it?'

'What? No, I don't think so.'

'It's the old Syndicate uniform,' says Suzanne. She is standing in the doorway with a long glass of amber-coloured liquid, holding it out for James.

'Ha,' says Aquila. The dress is cut low on Charity's breasts, tight to her waist. 'I don't remember them looking like that.'

'It's Sara's vision of the uniform. She likes to think of me as a Bounty Hunter, she said. Out there in the badlands, bringing in the skins of the flungouts.'

Aquila shifts in his chair. He doesn't like to talk about the End-of-Days.

Charity moves ceaselessly, circling the room, boasting about her display fight at Bacchanale, about her cover shoot for *Sneer*. Her empty glass dangles from her fingers. 'I was guest of honour at Seth Guleit's birth-day party. He fed me dragon fruit with his own hands. Seemed quite taken with me. He asked after you, Aquila: said you seemed to have gone into hibernation.'

Aquila nods. 'Seth always liked the city better than I did.'

'Not the way he tells it.'

'When's your first bout?' asks Suzanne.

'Two weeks. Torrador.'

They are all silent: Torrador, the Bull, is a solid, frightening wedge of muscle, hardly human.

'Will you be bulking up, a little, for that one?' Suzanne says, fiddling with her earring.

'Just a little, not much. My strength is my agility. I'll run rings around that side of ham.'

'Of course you will.' Aquila stands up, wavering only slightly. 'What say we eat, Suzanne? I'll help you get the things on the table.'

'Sure. Let's do that.'

Edward makes polite noises about helping them, which they politely refuse. As they're disappearing in the direction of the kitchen, Charity calls out, 'What about this cake? Can I see it?'

'In just a minute, sweetheart,' says Aquila. 'I have to put the – finishing touches on it.'

'He promised to make me a birthday cake,' she explains to Edward. 'By hand.'

'I didn't know people still did that. It's – adorable.'

'Isn't it?'

Charity takes another restless lap of the room. She

has so many building doses in her, speed doses, aggressors, she can only keep still for a little at a time. James watches her.

'And how are you, p'tit? You look a bit, what is it, pale? A bit thin?'

'I'm fine,' he says, looking away.

'Of course you are. Anyone would be pale, living in this house.'

'Don't you like it here?' says Edward. He has this habit, of asking her sudden, disconcerting questions.

'Oh, I like it fine,' she says. 'It's a triumph of design. Everyone says so. Shall I take you on a tour?'

'Sure.'

'Want to come, puppet?'

'Sure,' says James. He trots over and fits his hand in hers. They wander past the kitchen, where Aquila and Suzanne are bent over something or other, talking quietly, and down the long, wide, tranquil halls, soft ivory. Rooms open like big, calm flowers to each side: sitting rooms, a music room, a den with a conversation pit upholstered in Arctic-hued fur, and, at the end of the hall, a well-mannered waterfall that slips over wide lapping steps of cream stone.

'You see?'

'It's out of this world.'

'That's exactly what it is.'

In every room, walls of glass look out to nothing. 'In the day the views are quite wonderful. Aren't they, James? A kind of Nordic forest.'

'Birch trees.'

'Yes. This was my room.' She opens the door to show him. The room is a careful shrine, everything lined up just so, pictures of her in bounter gear, wild-eyed after a fight, holding trophies in the air.

Edward lingers, picking up a photograph of her, touching her yelling mouth. Charity puts a hand on the coverlet of her old bed. It's a pale cerulean patterned with snowflakes. It feels warm. She withdraws her hand.

'Let's go.'

'I want to see your toys,' says Edward. 'Are your old toys here?'

'I don't know. Let's go. James? Wouldn't you like to show us your room?'

'Okay.'

They go out into the hall. Edward takes Charity's hand in his own, and she gets that feeling he gives her, like she's walking in some long-ago countryside, with sunny skies and easy hills.

She remembers to breathe. This is the big thing, when she's dosed up for the start of the season, what they always tell her. She has to keep remembering to breathe, to stop and think before she takes things personally, to pause before screaming. To breathe. She will find herself gulping, struggling for air, and then remembers.

Every year the pharmas give her more, more. Every year it gets harder. Every year she wonders more who she is, and who she was. She feels like her chest is full of struggling eels. She is angry, angry. There's something fighting to get out of her. What is it? What is inside her?

James is tugging at her hand. 'Charity. Charity.' Edward is massaging her neck. 'Sweetheart. You okay?'

'Yeah. I'm fine. Why?'

They look at her, one on each side, her tiny brother, her lover with his liquid brown eyes, searching hers.

'I'm okay, I'm fine. Why don't we go and look at James's room? You'll like it, Edward. It's the nicest room in the house.'

'Do you really think that, Charity?' says James.

'I certainly do, munchkin. It's the nicest by far. Know why?'

'Why?'

'You live there. You make it the nicest. Because you're the nicest person in this house. By far.'

'Thank you.'

James's eyes are the biggest she's ever seen. Huge, luminous. Why is his face so thin? What does he want from her?

'Charity,' says Edward.

'What?'

'Do you remember what the pharmas told you? About the alcohol?'

'No, no, what?'

'They said there might be problems. With the new profile they have you on, they said any alcohol could maybe be a problem.'

'So why didn't you tell me? Why didn't you remind me when that bitch gave me the vodka? Why didn't you *stop* her, *kill* her? When it was me at stake?'

'Because she's your mother, Charity. And I thought you would be okay, because I'm here to look after you. And you are going to be okay. Because I'm here. I'm here.'

She feels the spent adrenaline prickle along her forearms. 'Oh God,' she says, 'oh God, I'm so sorry. Edward,' and she leans against him, helpless, 'I'm alright now. I'm sorry.'

He soothes wordless sounds into her ear.

James pulls his hand from hers and runs.

'Don't go! James, don't go!'

She can run so much faster than him, she can run so much faster than anyone in the whole world. She is at his door before he has taken more than a few paces.

'James! Don't! Don't be afraid!'

His eyes are so big, shining so strangely.

Edward walks into the small tight circle of them, her and the scared boy, and picks up James and rests him against his chest. He dandles him. And James almost immediately nestles against him, the crazed dilation of his eyes relaxes, he kicks his spindly ankles together, like a baby achieving a hard-fought sleep.

'Little man, you're okay, right? Yes. You're okay. And Charity's okay, aren't you, darling? So we're all okay. Now, shall we look at your room? I'd like to see it. I'm wondering what's in it. I'm thinking there's a nice cosy bed with a nice pillow. And a nice window. With a view of birch trees.'

'Yes,' whispers James, 'there are birch trees. Quiet.

Quiet trees.'

'I bet your room is the quietest room in the house. If you open the door real quick. And close it real quick.'

'Yes,' says James, closing his eyes ecstatically. 'That's right.'

'Shall we go and see?'

Charity opens the door. Edward, holding James, follows her in and closes the door. He puts the boy down.

She leans against him, exhausted, with a sense of narrow escape.

'You're fine, sweetheart,' he murmurs.

James sets off over the carpet, eager to display his kingdom. 'Look, Edward,' he says breathlessly.

'What is it?'

'Fish. My fish.'

James taps with his little frail fingernails against the bowl and the fish rise, humming, bubbling, singing in perfect harmony.

So pretty, striped like boiled lollies. Long swishy tails, film-star eyelashes, singing so sweetly. James measures out their powder solemnly, scatters it into the water. Then he trails his fingers against the clear, shining glass of the bowl, and the fish dance after them, following the pallid shine of his nails, leaping in adoration at the sound of his voice.

'What happens when you sing to them?' asks Edward.

James hides his face.

'Really, James, what happens? When no one else is here.'

'You sing, James?' says Charity in wonder. 'I've

never heard him sing,' she tells Edward.

'Listen. Listen.'

'I don't know if I can. I'm trying to be still, but I don't know if I can.'

Edward sits down against the cream wall. He seizes her and positions her between his thighs, squeezing her close.

James sings, as she could never have imagined he could sing, high, pure notes like struck crystal. The room fills with subtle vibrations. The song is something she's heard in the Old Quarter, a ballad from the End-of-Days.

'The vapour trails have faded . . . the sunflowers have set . . .'

The fat, stupid, uncontrollable tears run down her face.

'Don't cry, my darling,' whispers Edward. 'Listen.'

'You knew he could sing. How did you know? I would never have known, if you hadn't asked him. And I thought he was the thing I loved best in the world. The only thing I loved.'

'My precious. Don't cry.' He puts a hand on her back, in the tender zone the tissue therapists have identified, the one where she took her first injury. He curls her into him.

James sings, like the white swan of myth, while she sobs. And the fish leap from the bowl, they twirl around his outstretched fingers, they love him writhingly.

The song finishes and James stands in the middle of the room, bowing his head.

The fish settle in their bowl, humming.

'Thank you, James. Charity told me you were an artist. And I see, right away, that you are. I will remember that always. We both will.'

Charity does her best to hold her breath until she isn't her anymore, but it doesn't work. She still breathes, she still goes on feeling. She remembers Aquila glancing at her drawings, his careful saying of nothing, when she was as small as James. She remembers sitting on the stone steps at the dojo, her first year, both hands plunged into bowls of corrosive spirit, biting at her lips, watching the red peel back to white. *Flesh is weak*, said her master, *scars are strong*.

She goes on crying. She can't stop. And Edward, big and warm, holds her, contains the broken shell and spilling yolk of her.

'I like your pillow, James. Very delicate colour,' says Edward.

'Thanks.'

The boy comes close, cuddles between him and the weeping Charity, sheds his own tears. Edward opens his arms as far as they can go.

After a time Edward says in an undertone, 'Shall we go back?'

'What do you mean?'

'They'll be looking for us. And James. Shall we go back?'

'I don't want to go back.'

'I know, but I think maybe we should.'

Charity leans against the warmth of his chest.

'But I'm so comfortable here.'

'Me too,' whispers James.

'Wouldn't you like to see the cake? I would. I don't think I've ever seen a cake that someone's made with their own hands.'

'Yes, my cake,' says Charity. She sits up and scrubs her face with the heels of her hands. What is going on? Why has she been crying? This new profile is the worst yet. She can feel her heart rolling around in her chest like a ball of barbed wire, tearing fresh holes. She touches the control dangling between her breasts, the control for Edward's collar. It makes her feel better, to touch it.

James's face is red and blubbered.

'Why are you crying?' she asks him.

'I don't know. I'm scared.'

'Scared? Don't be silly. What are you scared of?'

He rolls onto his knees, keeping one hand on Edward, and doesn't answer her.

With a long, shaky sigh, Charity gets to her feet and looks at herself in the big round mirror on James's wall. Her face is burning, make-up smeared down her cheeks. Her scalp, newly shaved for the season, looks white and exposed.

'Great.'

She plucks a tissue from James's box and wipes away the sooty evidence of her tears, but her face still looks ravaged, smaller somehow, so completely unlike someone able to bout Torrador that she shudders with sudden fear.

This is ridiculous. She shouldn't be feeling fear,

not now. Not two weeks out. She should be feeling invincible.

The problem with Edward, who is supposed to keep her calm, is that he makes her feel things. Remember things. And then she is sitting on the floor crying, and she doesn't even know why.

She's not sure, actually, how the whole Edward thing is working out for her. He is, what would you call it, a double-edged sword.

She watches him in the mirror behind her, holding James on his knee. He knows how to handle everyone. It irritates her, sometimes, how easily he knows what to do.

'Why are you looking at me like that?' he says.

'I'm not. Like what? I'm not looking at you like anything.'

'You just looked – kind of angry.'

'I am angry. I am. I'm supposed to be. Have you ever seen him, Torrador? Size of a truck. I can't afford to be afraid. Not for a moment.'

'And you won't be. You'll be fine. You'll go in there and trounce him.'

'Yes. I will. I'll *grind* him.' She digs her heels into the carpet, picturing it. She plans to go for his tendons first thing, strip them out, cripple him, then circle him like a matador, taking pieces off him until he's broken at her feet.

Breathe, remember to breathe. She gulps, leans on the dresser.

Edward gets to his feet, placing James on the floor.

'Charity, I think we should go back to your parents now.'

'In a minute. Give me a minute.'

Edward takes a tissue and, holding James by the chin, cleans up his snotty face.

Charity looks into her own eyes.

I am not scared, she tells herself. *I am invincible. I am a machine. A machine.*

Everything soft in her must go. She has no need for it now.

10

The cake, once urgent, now seems beside the point. He and Suzanne face each other over the blackened mess of it, talking in low hisses. Suzanne is shaking all over, her arms braced against the bench.

'What is that thing?'

'I think I know. I've heard of them. A long time ago, when I was still buying the news, they were discussed as a possibility. I didn't know they could actually do it.'

'Do *what*? What is it?'

'It's called a simulian.'

'Is it, is it real?'

'What do you mean?'

'You know what I mean. Is it organic, is it a robot, what?'

'It's organic. Tube-grown.'

'But why? Why do they make them like that?' Suzanne is holding a knife, to smear frosting on the cake, but it quivers in her hand, forgotten.

'It's easier. To use simian genes. It's easier to grow or something. Or maybe easier to control, afterwards. I can't remember exactly.'

'But he talks like a human. They must have done something to his tongue.'

'There's human DNA in there. He has some human . . . parts.'

'Oh my God, she lets this thing . . . she has sex with it?'

'I don't know. You can, I suppose. It's possible.'

'It's an outrage. It's disgusting.'

'That's a little old-fashioned of you, don't you think? You've never used a joystick, Suzanne?'

She flushes. 'That's completely different. They're machines. She treats this thing like her boyfriend. That's what she called him, on the phone to James. Her boyfriend. And she didn't even warn us.'

'Yes, that was unfair.'

'Very happy together! That's what she said. Is she insane?' Suzanne's eyes dart to the doorway.

'Where did she get it?' says Aquila. 'That's what I want to know.'

'What do you mean? She bought it. She must have.'

'I don't know about that. I don't think you can buy them on the open market. Not yet.'

'I can't do this,' says Suzanne.

Aquila grabs her wrist. 'You have to. You don't have a choice.'

'Pretend like he's her boyfriend? Pretend we notice nothing?'

'Evidently that's how she wants to play it.'

Suzanne pulls her hand away. 'What can be going through her head?'

'You know what she's like. Especially when she starts getting dosed up for the season.'

'But she seems – calm. Calmer. She hasn't screamed once. She seems – happy.'

'That's what she said. That she's happy.'

'With this, this thing? This ape in a suit?'

'It has a collar. Did you see? Some kind of control, it looks like.'

'It scares me.'

He laughs. 'Why? Don't you think Charity would be a match for him, if something went wrong?'

'I'm not sure. He's huge. Those teeth. Those pointed teeth.' She shudders.

'And yet, he's very gentle. Very soft-spoken, very polite.'

'But he's an ape. What makes him like that, the collar?'

'Maybe. Programming? Implanting? I don't know.'

Suzanne presses her fingers to her temples. 'But this can't go on and on. Surely she doesn't really mean to keep him with her like a boyfriend. It's a whim. She's too used to buying her pleasures.'

'We'll see. For now, let's get through tonight. For instance, how do we fix this?'

Together they survey the ruin of the cake, which is lumpen, misshapen, caved in at the middle, black on the top.

'We can't let her see it like this,' says Suzanne. 'It might set her off.'

'So what do we do?'

'Ice it. Cover it up with frosting. And fast. She'll be getting restless.'

'Where is she? I can't hear them.'

Suzanne creeps to the door.

'They're not there. She must be showing him something, her room maybe. The pictures.'

'How touching.'

'It's grotesque.'

'James?' says Aquila.

'He must be with them. I don't like that.'

'He'll be okay. Charity would never let anything happen to him.'

'It just makes me uneasy.'

'Come on. The frosting. And her name, we have to put her name on it.'

They work feverishly, following another recipe gleaned from Arkhive. This bit is easier: sugar, water, a paste. It works, although it's maybe a little sloppy. He slaps it over the cracks, fills the depression in the centre. The cachous sink when they first try to put them on: they wait, Suzanne gnawing at her nails, until it hardens, and manage to spell her name.

'Something about love?'

'Not enough left. I dropped some.' His lumbar twinges at the memory of crawling under the bed.

'I think it looks alright now. Not great, but alright. We might scrape through.'

The smart waiter chirrups. The first course, a complicated, flamingo-coloured soup with a flourish of herbs and flowers in the centre, is ready to go.

'Help me with this.'

They set the soup in the dining room and stand around nervously.

'What about him? There aren't enough bowls.'

'Give him mine,' says Suzanne. 'I'm not hungry.'

As they are arguing about who should go to summon the others, Charity strides in the door.

'Okay, then, let's eat.'

—

'You sit here, and – Edward –'

'Thank you, Suzanne.'

Edward grins at her, showing the sharp simian teeth.

'Do you like soup? Edward?'

'I like soup very much, yes.'

They sit. Bach cantatas spill soothingly from the ceiling. They watch each other, they pick up their spoons. Charity looks hard and burnished, glances around as if daring them all. James looks shaky. Edward smiles, and despite herself, Suzanne relaxes. Despite herself, she feels a gratitude towards this thing. Charity's birthday parties have never gone this well.

They drink the pretty soup.

'Nasturtium,' says Edward approvingly, and pops the flower in his mouth. 'Aren't you having any, Suzanne?'

Suzanne shrugs. 'I don't think I will, darling.

I don't go in for food very much. Give me a shake, a dose, I'm happy.'

She leans on one elbow, her chin in her hand.

'But it's wonderful, isn't it? To experience these tastes, textures, colours?' Edward holds up his spoon, examining the neon pool within it.

'It's an illusion,' says Suzanne in a hard voice.

'Yes. But so much is, no?'

'That's the truth,' says Suzanne, unable to restrain a cackle.

'Some things are real,' says Charity icily.

'Oh yes? Isn't it marvellous you can tell.'

They all avoid looking at Edward, who takes another measured spoonful of his soup.

'Be quiet, Suzanne,' says Aquila in a low voice.

'I won't.'

They glare at each other.

James says wearily, 'Stop it, can't you?' and everyone looks at him in amazement.

'You make me tired,' he says.

'I know how you feel,' says Suzanne.

'Stop,' says Aquila.

'Suzanne,' says Edward, 'let me help you with these soup bowls. I think everyone's finished.'

She sits for a minute, then flings down her napkin and gets up. 'Fine, Edward. Thank you.'

They take out the bowls.

'It's interesting, isn't it,' says Charity.

'What is, sweet?'

'How she got like this. She couldn't always have been

like this, or you would never have married her. Or was she just, I don't know, fantastic at sucking your cock?'

'Please.'

'Well? What was it? When did she turn?'

Aquila tilts his head, as if paying particular attention to the geometry of the Bach. 'She didn't "turn". Everything is fine. She's just a little drunk. A little tired. Like she said.'

'She's not *tired*. This has been going on for years.'

'She's sad,' says James.

'She's not sad. What does she have to be sad about?' says Aquila.

'She cries.'

'Well, we all cry, sometimes.'

'Really?' says Charity. 'What do you cry about?'

'I don't know. Things. Sometimes.'

A pause. The slow, imperceptible growth of the centrepiece, every second more vividly red, a little nearer the ceiling.

'Let's talk about your face, shall we?'

'Must we? It's not a pleasant story.'

'I think I would enjoy it.'

Aquila looks meditatively at the ceiling. 'I was in the city.'

'That's not like you.'

'I was getting the ingredients for your cake. Some of them were difficult to lay hands on.'

'How sweet of you to go to all that effort. And? You got – mugged?'

'In a way. Attacked.'

'By who?'

'A fan. I think.'

'A woman?'

'Yes,' says Aquila, after a beat.

'I can tell.'

'If anyone can, you can, sugar-pie.'

'Exactly. So, a fan. I thought it might be Antoinette. I hear she has a bit of a temper.'

'What?' Aquila stiffens.

'You think I don't know about her? It's common knowledge. You can't blame her, really, can you? Suzanne, I mean. You kind of made her what she is, don't you think?'

Suzanne and Edward edge their way into the room, laden with dishes.

'What is this?' asks Aquila smoothly.

'Dugong. Done in the Wellington style.'

'Marvellous. How exotic.'

'Tuck in!' says Suzanne, with a nautical flourish of her hand.

After a little, it becomes apparent that Edward is not eating.

'You're not hungry?' says Suzanne.

'Forgive me. I don't think it would agree with me.'

'I told you he wouldn't eat much,' says Charity.

'Why don't you eat, Edward?' says James.

'I do, little one. But I can only eat certain things. It's the way I'm built.'

'What things?'

'Oh, you know. Leaves, pith, algae. Larvae, honey.

Flying squirrels.'

'Flying squirrels. He loves them,' says Charity.

'What an interesting diet,' says Aquila.

'Edward is a bonobo,' says Suzanne. 'Primarily. He was telling me in the kitchen.' She rubs his arm fondly.

'Primarily?' says Aquila.

Edward touches his throat. 'Bonobo mainly. A little gorilla. A little homo sapiens.'

'What's a bonobo?' says James.

'It's a simian.' Charity leans back in her chair, her eyes watchful. 'Dwarf or gracile chimpanzee.'

'Nothing dwarf about Edward,' says Suzanne.

'I get my height and heft from my gorilla blood.'

'Blood?' says Aquila.

'Yes,' says Edward. He lounges in his seat, at ease.

'When is *your* birthday?' Aquila asks him.

'I don't know.'

'Do you remember? Being born?'

'No,' says Edward evenly. 'Do you?'

'Obviously not.'

'Obviously.'

'Who raised you?'

'I don't know.'

'What's your first memory?'

'Charity.'

There is a silence.

'Isn't that touching,' says Aquila. He takes a bite of the dugong, chews.

'It's quite something,' says Charity, 'to be loved like that.'

'What's that thing around your neck, Edward?' says Aquila.

Edward touches his collar, glances at Charity.

'It's just in case,' she says.

'In case what?'

'I have the control. In case Edward forgets.'

'Forgets what?'

'Who he is.'

The dugong congeals on the plates.

'Why would I forget that?' says Edward. 'How could I forget?'

'I don't know. They told me to carry it. So I do.' Charity plucks the pendant from her cleavage and holds it up. 'There's a button. I can press it. If I need to.'

Edward's heavy brow lowers.

'They?' says Aquila. 'Where did you get this – Edward? Who gave him to you?'

'He's been assigned to me. By the Syndicate.'

'The Syndicate find you – boyfriends – now?'

'Why not? They know what suits me best. They know what I need.'

'And what is that?'

'Edward,' says Charity, with a QED flourish.

Aquila stares at her.

'I like Edward,' says James.

'I do too,' says Suzanne. 'Edward is wonderful.'

Aquila turns to Edward, his mouth set in his most charming smile. 'You certainly have the ability to win hearts.'

'Your family is very special,' Edward says.

'Aren't they? Yes, aren't they unique?'

'I don't think I've ever seen anything like this house. This family.'

'But then, you can't have seen very much at all, can you?'

'That's where you're wrong,' says Charity. 'Edward has extensive memories. Many experiences.'

'Does he? How?'

'It's the way he's built.'

'But how, Charity? How does it work?'

'I don't know. I don't care, I don't need to know.'

Aquila slaps his hand on the table. 'Tell us, then, Edward. What do you remember?'

'What kind of question is that?' says Charity. 'What do you remember, Aquila?'

Edward smiles at her across the table. 'I know what he means.'

'I know what he means too,' says Charity.

'It's natural to be curious. Alright, Aquila, I remember lives, animal lives, human lives, whole towering forests, birds, rain, love.'

Suzanne brings her glass, quivering, to her lips; her eyes brim.

'How can you possibly,' says Aquila in a low voice.

'Does it matter? I remember. I feel it. Sweet mango that ran down my chin.'

'Do you have dreams?' Suzanne asks. She leans towards him, her head almost touching his shoulder.

'Yes.'

'You don't take dose?' Aquila says sharply.

'No. No need.'

'No *need*?'

'Why don't you shut up?' says Charity. Her eyes are unfixed, flinty. She holds her fork still, the tines down, and Aquila pays sudden attention to her.

'You know what, Charity? Charity? Maybe it's time for presents.'

'Yes,' says Charity. She drags her hand over her mouth, wiping spittle. 'Presents.'

Suzanne snaps her head away from Edward's shoulder. 'I'll get you one. Or do you want to choose yourself? Look, there's a whole mountain of them.'

'No,' says Charity, her head weaving like a bull's. 'I want James to open his present.'

They all glance at James, who sits, white and little and forgotten, at the foot of the table.

'Where is it?' says Suzanne.

Charity glares into the corners of the room, stands too fast, knocking her plate of dugong; it flips, dumping its contents on the carpet. No one says anything, or moves.

'Your bag?' says Edward. 'I remember you put it down by the lift.'

'Thank you, Edward. Always paying attention.' In one charged bound, Charity leaves the room. In blinktime she's back again, landing by James's chair with knife precision. He flinches.

'What do *you* remember, James?' she asks him, speaking so softly they can hardly hear her. 'Do you remember the stories I used to tell you, when you were only a baby?'

'How could I remember? I was only a baby.'

'Some people remember. When they were a baby. What happened, how they were born.'

'That's not true,' says Aquila.

'Careful,' Suzanne breathes.

Charity lifts her chin, scornful. 'I am talking. With James. Who is the nicest person in this house. By far.'

Suzanne and Aquila exchange a glance.

'Anyway, puppet, here's your present. Will you open it now?'

'Yes,' says James. Charity relaxes her fist, revealing a small bonbon of a present with glacé ribbon and reflective paper.

'It's beautiful,' James says.

'That's just the wrapping, silly. Open it, quick!' Unable to wait for him, she tears the paper, and he gasps. Something falls to the floor.

Charity curses. 'My motor coordination is all out. This profile is useless. I'm gonna tear those pharmas into mince.'

James dives under the table and comes up with the gift balanced on his palm, his eyes widening.

'What is it?' he says.

'I don't actually know.' Charity bursts out laughing and sits back on her heels. 'I bought it from some ancient in the Old Quarter. I've never seen anyone so old. He had wrinkles on his throat, hair in his ears. He was selling these from a bandolier.'

'What is it, James?' says Aquila.

James holds it up. 'A man?'

'What is he standing on?' Suzanne comes to see. 'He's on the top of a train.'

'What's a train?' says James.

'It's something that carried people through tunnels, like a big catazoom.'

'Or through the open,' says Edward, 'through mountains, across deserts.'

'What's that on his shoulder?' says James.

'A cat,' says Charity. 'See its green eyes?'

'I would like a cat,' says James.

They all laugh. Suzanne says, 'Sweetie, fish are all we can manage. Cats are for, well . . .'

'Squillionaires,' says Aquila.

'Even then. They're very rare. The hardest thing of all to replicate, they say.'

'Is he a squillionaire?' says James. He squints at the figurine.

'I don't know. He doesn't look like one.' Suzanne holds him up to the light. 'He seems to be wearing no shirt. Just a kind of a fur – what would you say? Jerkin?'

'Let me see this fellow,' says Aquila.

'No,' says James. 'It's my present. I want to hold it.'

'That's right, p'tit,' says Charity. 'We can't let him take everything. Can we.'

'Shall we have pudding now, Suzanne?' says Aquila. 'Shall I help you?'

'Edward will help me.'

'Edward will? How nice of him. How – helpful.'

Edward stands. Looms. In this room, with its

ceiling spun gold with baroque barcaroles and subtle downlights, he seems particularly large.

'Shall we?' He offers Suzanne his hand.

'Don't be long, doll,' says Charity.

'Of course I won't. I'll be just a minute.'

'Good.'

James balances the figurine on the edge of his untouched plate. Charity says, 'Why aren't you eating anything?'

'I am.'

'No. I haven't seen you eat a thing all night. And you're thin. You're as thin as a bit of paper.'

'Children are often thin.'

'I wasn't talking to you, Aquila. Let him answer. James?'

'I eat,' he says.

'What was the last thing you ate?'

James considers; he makes the figurine circle his plate.

'Do you have your foodshake in the morning?'

'Yes.'

'At night?'

'Yes. Mostly.'

'Aren't you hungry, puppet?' Charity strokes his hair, a little hard: he shrinks into himself.

'Not really.'

'Why? When I was your age I ate everything I could get my hands on.'

'Don't forget the doses you were on,' says Aquila.

'I'm not likely to forget that, am I?'

'Dear heart.'

'Whose dear heart? You assessed me. You found me lacking. Isn't that right? And then you made me what I am today.'

'Not lacking . . . just . . . different.'

'Not fit to follow in your footsteps, isn't that right?'

'You made your own footsteps. And look at you.'

'You made me.'

'We saw your potential. And we had advice.'

'I was six years old. You couldn't have waited? You couldn't have given me time to develop, taught me?' Charity's fingers twine around themselves, the knuckles white.

'We've been over this, sweet. It can't be taught.'

'So you cut me loose.'

'We hardly "cut you loose", Charity. We nurtured your potential. And look at you, look at what you've become. You're a champion. Unbeatable.'

'Yes.' Charity fits her palms together: her muscles flow into a perfect, cut symmetry. 'There's not much I can't do, physically. Maybe I should even be pleased. James here, your darling, your protégé, your heir, your apple's eye, he don't look too well. Maybe I should be pleased I escaped your special attention.'

'Charity,' says Aquila, 'you always had my special attention.'

'Daddy's girl,' she mocks.

'Weren't you?'

'Once.'

'Yes. Once.'

In the silence that follows, all that can be heard is

the tiny wheels of James's figurine, circling and circling the ruins of the dugong.

—

'Cloudberry parfait,' trills Suzanne. She and Edward come into the room, bearing trays with tall fluted glasses. The handles of the long spoons are frosted, as if with light snow. The glasses are clear, dark, glowing red, like venous blood.

'Cloudberry,' says Edward. 'I'd never heard of it before. Suzanne has been telling me.' He crosses to Charity and touches the sheen of sweat on her face. 'You want some, honey? Parfait?'

'Yes. We'll all have some. Won't we. James? Let's eat some.'

'Okay,' says James. He takes the glass, but has trouble wielding the long spoon.

'Here,' says Edward. He takes the spoon and offers James a red mouthful. James opens his mouth willingly; he takes spoonful after spoonful from Edward, staring at him adoringly.

'Well, look at that,' says Charity.

'It's delicious,' says Edward. 'Sweet. Cool. Try some.'

'I think I will.'

'It's not quite the same, of course, as the real ones,' says Suzanne.

Edward looks at her. 'The real ones?'

'The real cloudberries. I had them once, way back.

In the Old Quarter. Before the dome, before it was sealed over. Before it became the – amusement park, the museum – that it is today.'

'Suzanne comes from the Old Quarter,' Charity tells Edward.

'Charity,' says Aquila.

'What? She did, she does. Are you ashamed of it?'

'Of course not.'

'My father,' Charity tells Edward, 'was rather fond of slumming it. In his youth.'

'Stop it,' says Aquila.

All of them look at Suzanne, who seems oblivious, staring into the air beyond them. 'I had the cloudberries at the fish market,' she says. 'There was a man who sold salmon. He was from Finland.'

'Finland,' says James, experimenting with the sound. 'Were there fish there?'

'There were fish everywhere. In the sea,' says Edward. 'The water. The great, rolling water.'

Suzanne and James turn to him with an identical look of wonder.

Charity upends her empty glass on the table, making a red mark on the pristine cloth. 'Well, that's dinner. Now what?'

'Presents?' says Aquila.

Aquila. Aquila. The susurration of the phone.

'Ignore it,' he says.

'Why?' says Charity.

'It will wait. It's your birthday.'

'Precisely. And I think you should take it. So . . .?'

Aquila sits, impassive.

'Take it,' says Suzanne. She gets up and runs her hand impatiently over the lens. It clears to show Heide's eager face.

'Suzanne? Is Aquila there? I'm so sorry, I didn't mean to –'

'What is it?' snaps Aquila.

'It's important, or I wouldn't have –'

'What, Heide? Make it fast.'

'I've got buyers. For the sculpture. It's a consortium, they're willing to take the whole run. But they want to see it right away.'

'Not possible.'

'It's unheard of, Aquila. The whole run. But they must see it tonight.'

'I'm busy. Charity's birthday, I told you.'

'Yes, I understand . . . Charity, I'm so sorry . . . but –'

'Sculpture, huh?' says Charity. 'Maybe we should all see it.'

'No,' says Aquila.

'Where is it? The basement?'

'It's not ready.'

'You said it was finished,' says Suzanne.

'Aquila, I understood it was finished,' said Heide. 'I have major buyers here. They're waiting to link in.'

'Later. After Charity's birthday.'

'I can hold them off until midnight tonight. No longer.'

'I'll call you back before then. We'll talk.'

'I'm sorry to intrude, really. But this is big, I had to let you know . . .' Heide's voice fades; the lens darkens.

'I'm sorry,' says Aquila.

Charity shrugs. 'The penalties of having a famous father.'

'I'm not so famous. Compared to you.'

'It's a different kind of fame. Isn't it. So, what's this sculpture? A big work? Like *Scraper Canyon*?'

'Apparently,' says Suzanne, 'it's not like anything else.'

'Why all the mystery?' says Charity.

'Wouldn't you rather have presents? Cake?'

'Afterwards. I want to see this thing. Come on, Aquila. Stop holding out.'

'You come down, sweet pea. The rest don't have to see it.'

'But I want Edward to come.'

Aquila rubs a hand over his face. 'Very well. If you really want.'

'I really want.' Charity throws her napkin on the floor and stands, pulling herself to her full height, flexing this way and that, suddenly seeming very pleased about something.

Aquila strides out of the room and they all follow him, Suzanne stumbling a little in her high heels, Edward with his hand fitted to the curve of Charity's back, James last, the figurine dangling from his hand.

11

Wide whitewashed steps lead down into the basement, which is subtly lit, harbouring pools of
shadow, until Aquila taps a console and the arc lights
blare out. Everyone winces.

'You need this light,' he explains. 'To work. To see.'
His face feels raw and exposed.

The basement is empty except for the vast crouched
shape squatting in its centre, concealed by a dust sheet.
All his other works are sold, in houses, in museums and
public buildings, performing their civic duties, easing
the passage of lives.

The thing is enormous, at least three times Aquila's
height. He'd had to use the ceiling wires to make it.
For a moment he thinks he won't be able to get the
sheet off, especially when it catches on a protuber-
ance, but in the end (in the process tearing, it feels,
one or two of his major ligaments, perhaps a sinew or

two) he manages it. And there it is.

He had seen it only that morning, but it is already a shock.

'I don't believe it,' says Suzanne.

'I do,' says Charity. She comes down the stairs in a rush and for a moment he cowers, to his shame, against the sculpture, but it seems she is only taking a closer look.

Edward is frozen against the wall. Suzanne, behind him, puts a hand on his shoulder.

'He didn't know,' she tells him.

'He must have,' he says.

'No. It was as much of a shock to him, when you turned up – I mean –'

'I know what you mean.'

James comes up in his quiet way behind the sim-ulian, takes hold of his massive leg behind the knee, and leans against him, looking down at the work.

'It's not like you,' he says. 'Not really.'

Edward looks down at him briefly. 'I know.'

Charity is circling the work, running her hands over it. Suzanne creeps down another step, hesitating, holding her skirts, as if descending into a pool of chill water.

The sculpture is an immense ape made from blackened wood. It crouches, clutching its stiffened cock. Its head is hunkered into its body, its mouth open in a rictus of pain: two long, jagged sticks pierce the base of its neck. The modelling is rudimentary. The thing seems made from hulking blocks, splintered roughly against each other, as if they've been forced together by a powerful impact.

Edward sits down on the stairs and rests his chin on his hand, staring at the thing.

James sinks to his knees. He looks back at the heavy door, which has closed with its own quiet weight.

'Edward,' he whispers, but the simulian doesn't answer him.

'What did you mean by this, Aquila?' he asks.

'Mean? I meant nothing.'

'Doesn't art mean something? Weren't you thinking of something, when you made it? You must have been, to imprint the membrane.'

Aquila doesn't know where it came from. Usually when he works he's like a pilot in the harness, suavely in control, directing the impulses. When he'd made this – and it took some time, it required him to return to it again and again – he'd been like a passenger, helpless. The harness had sawed at his back; his hands had moved recklessly, trembling. His mind had been crowded with images. He'd worked until he was nauseous with exhaustion.

'I wasn't thinking at all, really. It was more that I was – seeing something.'

'Wait,' says Charity. 'What is wrong with James?'

They all look to where she's pointing, to where James, buckled on the stairs, has begun to curl inwards on himself, his hands agonised claws, his legs twisting around each other.

The lights dim, flicker, then resume their merciless glare.

Suzanne kicks off her shoes and runs up the stairs.

Edward drops his head, as if finding it suddenly heavy. 'I am sorry, goddess,' he says, and all the lights go out.

—

Blackness.

Blackness so complete they are only sounds to each other. Suzanne, it seems, has tripped on her headlong rush up the stairs; she falls with a swish and a thump and is silent. James wheezes with a sound like dry leaves swept on a path. Charity swears in a low, guttural voice. Aquila is pressed, shocked, against the black hunk of wood. His mind crouches in its skull, waiting. There is a tearing, then a clatter of metal on the floor. It's the sound of Edward ridding himself of his collar. How does he know that, without being able to see?

Charity hisses, snarls, the way bounters do when they begin their fights.

The wind of Edward's coming is the first he knows of his attack. A buffeting wave of air is the first thing to knock him down, and probably saves his life, because it means that Edward misjudges his spring and overshoots. Aquila is merely struck a glancing blow by one of the colossal legs, which is still enough to send him rolling over and over on the floor.

'Edward!' screams Charity, and he can't believe she's betrayed her position, until he realises that she has done it, incredibly, for him.

There are several sickening thuds, a bellow, and

the sound of the ape bounding up the stairs to collide with the basement door, a crash that shakes the walls. And again. And again, until the stubborn door (soundproofing, humidity-controlling, Aquila's way of locking out the world) gives for a moment, offering a second's sight of the silhouetted ape achieving its freedom.

—

The house is silent.

When they reach the hall, Aquila, staggering under the weight of Suzanne, asks Charity to try the touch lights.

'Nothing,' she says. 'The grid is down.'

'But they must be doing something. They must be fixing it. How could this happen?'

'There was always the danger that the dome could rupture. It could be as simple as a container spinning off a ship as it comes into the atmosphere. Smack. Or it could be an attack. Flungouts.'

Aquila lays Suzanne on the carpet. 'That's just some stupid rumour. There's no one outside. The Bounty Hunters brought them all in, years ago. And if any escaped, how could they live in the air?'

'Maybe they found somewhere uncontaminated to live. There have been rumours in the city for years.'

'I don't believe it. That's the kind of carnie talk you hear in the Old Quarter when they try to sell you hero figures. Like that thing you bought James.'

He kneels and puts his hand on James's head,

running his fine corn-silk hair through his fingers. 'Wake up, youngling,' he whispers.

James blows a bubble.

Suzanne kicks her legs and moans. Aquila bends over her. In the gloom of the unlit house, all he can see of her is a mass of pale hair and a white oval with a dark mouth.

'You fell,' he says.

'I know that. There was something – James.'

'Yes, he's here.'

'Where is Edward?' she whispers.

'Edward – took his collar off,' says Aquila. 'Apparently it was run off the grid, which seems to be down right now. He became violent.'

'But he wouldn't hurt us. Not Charity. Not James.'

'Like hell he wouldn't hurt me,' snarls Charity. 'I'm carrying at least two broken ribs and I've got a bite to my shoulder that I'm just lucky he didn't get a real grip on. I got his windpipe. He'll be a very sorry ape tonight.'

'How could that be? Not Edward. He was so . . .'

'He was his collar.'

Suzanne touches her temple. 'Ugh. I hurt. Give me James. Let me check him.'

Aquila hesitates, then picks up the squirming James and delivers him to Suzanne, who feels him, alarmed.

'He's all wet.'

'It's – spit.'

'He's all crooked!'

'Yes.'

'What's wrong with him?'

'Let's talk about it later.'

'Aquila, you're scaring me. Tell me *right now* what is wrong with James.'

'Okay.' He takes her hand. She pulls it away.

'Listen, Suzanne. Something has happened out there. The grid is down. The house, the house without the grid . . .'

'I give it twenty-four hours before it unforms,' says Charity.

'Surely longer. Surely.' He looks around at the looming walls, their solidity. The waterfall is still running, the sound of it eerie in the dark.

'James,' says Suzanne, holding her chest as she coughs. 'Tell me.'

How does he tell her? After all this time?

'Without the house, James is – he's different. He's not like us.'

'Nonsense,' says Suzanne. 'Of course he is. What are you talking about?'

'I know you don't remember this. Because you asked not to. He was born with palsy.'

'What? What is that?'

'It's a disease. It causes – faults.'

'I don't believe you.' Suzanne cuddles James closer. 'How could they have let him be born if he had a disease?'

'These things happen. The screenings aren't perfect. Usually you can't tell he has it, because of the grid. He has an implant. And if you have a very powerful draw, like this house has, like I need to have for the harness, then it's controlled. With the implant, James could be like any other boy.'

'He's not like any other boy,' says Suzanne, her voice cracking.

'I know.'

'Faults?' says Charity. 'What faults?'

'I'm not even sure. I didn't have to know, because James was safe here. Things like – slurred speech. Crossed eyes. Paralysis.'

'His mind?'

'It doesn't affect the mind.'

'Is he awake? Can he hear us?'

'I don't know,' says Aquila. He puts his hand on James's head.

'What do you mean, I asked not to remember?' says Suzanne.

'You had it built into your dose. You didn't want to know about it.'

Charity shakes her head.

'And you did?' Suzanne asks Aquila.

'I thought it was best that one of us did. Just in case something happened.'

Suzanne makes it to all fours, craning over James. 'I can't see. I can't *see properly*.'

'Wait,' says Charity. 'Wait until daylight.'

'Is there daylight? Will there be?'

'We'll find out, I guess.'

Suzanne lies next to James and draws him against her body. 'He still has that man in his hand. Your present, that man with the cat.' She cradles him into her, wrapping around him, crying softly into his hair.

'Sleep, if you want to,' says Charity to Aquila. 'I won't.'

He gets pillows and coverlets from his bedroom, which is closest, and he, Suzanne and James bed down in the hallway. Somehow he doesn't want to go into the rooms, which are cobwebbed with shadow. Without its small confiding hums and chirrups the house seems hostile, churlishly silent. He listens to the pad of Charity's feet and Suzanne's whimpers and tries not to think of the thing below them in the basement, its teeth bared to the dark.

PART TWO: BLACK-BEAKED BIRDS

12

Through the skylights, through the picture windows in the bedrooms, through the wall-length panes of glass at each end of the hallway, comes the thuggish sun.

Charity stands at one of the hallway windows, a knife dangling loose in one hand, the other perched on her hip. The birch trees, the snowdrops and jonquils at their roots, the low hills, the blond grasses, the parchment skies are gone. The frames of the trees are dissolving, dripping long globular beads on the arid ground.

Suzanne winces awake.

'God, what is that?'

'The sun,' says Charity.

'I don't remember it being like that.' Suzanne covers her eyes, pressing: her vision reels and bursts with red stars.

'The dome has split,' says Charity.

Aquila is still sleeping, his head in a shadowed corner.

Suzanne sucks in a breath and looks at James.

He's lying curled where she left him, still in the shape of her body. With his hair over his face he looks as if he's in his own bed, the way he looks when she creeps in at night. Gently, sick in the pit of her belly, she smooths the hair back.

He doesn't look so bad, still has a nose and mouth, still has those hazel eyes, so clear you can look inside them, into their complicated pattern. But he doesn't look back at her. His eyes are skewed, rolling in odd directions. His mouth, so delicately set, holding himself always away from them, holding himself in, lolls open. His head flops. His hand grips the figurine Charity gave him.

'Remember he said he wanted a cat,' says Charity.

'He loves animals. Books with animals in them were always his favourites.'

Her mind skitters. The daylight means dose. But there is no dose.

The house, in the bald sunlight, looks bleached and lifeless. The lenses have lost their lustrous, mercurial glow. The resins are dull. The windows are like dead eyes, open to the sky. She gets to her feet and wanders into the kitchen. It glitters like a knife, blinding her. She feels for the little smoked-glass clamshell of the dose-maid. Stubbornly shut. Her long nails slide uselessly down it.

'Suzanne, there's no dose,' says Charity from the

doorway. 'There's no food, no clothes, nothing coming from the city. The house is finished.'

'What do we do?'

'Eventually, we leave.'

'But the air!'

'We don't have a choice. The safe air in here will be gone soon.'

'But Charity. The air will kill us.'

'We're dead anyway if we stay.' Charity's face is cold and composed, that of a fighter in fight mode, weighing options.

'How can you be so calm?'

'You just wait until my profile wears off,' says Charity. She smiles maniacally and leaves the room. Suzanne lingers a little. If she closes her eyes she can recreate for a moment the dazed mornings she spent here, before anyone woke, waiting for the dose-maid to open and serenade her, listening to the bright, steady murmurs of the house.

Charity strides from end to end of the hall, checking the windows, checking James. Aquila, incredibly, is still sleeping, his hands clutched boyishly between his thighs.

Suzanne appears in the doorway.

'We should wake him,' she says, gesturing towards Aquila.

'Be my guest.'

Suzanne stands over him, then reconsiders, kneels.

'Aquila.'

'It's not ready yet,' he says fretfully.

'*Aquila*. It's morning.'

'Not yet.' He opens his eyes, sees her, and blinks in confusion, wiping spit from his jaw. 'Everything's safe? Edward didn't come back?'

'Edward is probably half dead in some convenient stretch of wasteland,' says Charity.

'That's my girl,' says Aquila. He sits up, his face creasing with pain. 'God. This morning hurts.'

'Welcome to life without dose,' says Charity.

Aquila looks up at her. 'You okay? You should have had a profile dose by now, right?'

'I should have had four. I was waking up for them every three hours, before. Feel a bit like I'm going to throw up.'

'Thanks for watching us. For not sleeping.'

'Aren't you glad now your little girl wasn't an artist?'

'Not particularly. Actually, I always thought you would be. When you were a baby. I don't know, you had such piercing eyes. Like you could see through things.'

'Well, maybe you screwed it up,' says Charity, clenching and unclenching her hands, the perfect muscles under her collarbones streaming like water. 'Maybe I was supposed to be, and you screwed it up somehow.'

'Maybe,' says Aquila. 'God knows we screwed up everything else.'

Charity squints her eyes against the sun. 'You two seen out here?'

'No.' Truth to tell, Suzanne has been avoiding the windows.

Aquila sighs and gets up. He and Suzanne peer out at the melting skeletons of the trees.

'Everything in here will start to unform as well,' says Charity.

'How soon?'

'Who knows? A day or so. Especially with the sun coming in like this. I suppose even our clothes, soon.'

Suzanne looks incredulously around her. This cool, obliging shell has always seemed inviolate. But it's no more than a gingerbread house, after all. Her gown feels suddenly limp and slimy.

'You see that?' Charity points to the horizon.

'What?' Suzanne's eyes are not up to Charity's bounter-trained and dose-boosted vision.

'It's the city. I can see smoke.'

Aquila turns his face away. All his works, his precious works.

'We can't go that way.' Charity taps the knife against the glass. 'It will be pandemonium in there.'

'But there isn't another way.' Aquila goes to the western windows. Nothing. Bare, hopeless rock, ending in shimmer.

'Maybe we can get help in the city,' says Suzanne. 'For James, for ourselves. There will be hospitals. You're hurt.' She indicates Charity's shoulder, which is dirty, torn, looks chewed.

'Don't you understand what it will be like?' says Charity.

'At least everyone will be in the same predicament.'

'Everyone will be in the same stinking sinkhole.

And clawing to stand on each other's faces. Don't you get what is happening here? The dome has ruptured. It's the End-of-Days. Again.'

'That didn't work out so bad, as it happens,' says Aquila. 'I have money. You have money.'

'We have credit cards. Which is now another way of saying, we have nothing.'

'I know people.' For the first time he thinks, painfully, of Antoinette.

'Who are possibly already dead. Or even if they're alive, the last thing on their mind is going to be kowtowing to Masterful You for your deft use of the colour wheel.' Charity frowns down at her wound, plucking a frilled edge of flesh.

'What's the alternative?'

'The only advantage we have is that we're so far away from the city. We're close to the edge of the dome, or where the dome was. Whatever is outside starts that much closer to where we are. We have a head start.'

'What are you talking about?' Aquila beats on the glass. 'This is what is outside the dome. Endless rock, endless heat. You think there is a promised land out there?'

'Well, don't worry about it too much.' Charity gazes at the wasteland. 'The air will probably kill us in a couple of days.'

'She's right, Aquila,' says Suzanne. 'We know the distance to the city. We'd die trying to walk it. At least her way, there's a kind of . . . thrill of the unknown.' She gives a snort of laughter.

'You are both mad,' Aquila says. 'But we can hardly split up.'

'Yes, it's a little late to divorce us now,' Charity says. She is tiring, he sees: sagging against the glass, the knife limp in her fist.

He takes her, for the first time in her adult life, in his arms. 'Rest.'

She steps back, glowering.

'You know you need to.'

Charity looks down at her torn and bloodied dress. She shrugs and turns to Aquila, presenting her shaven nape.

'Can you unzip me?'

Bewildered, shaken, he does it.

'I guess I am kind of tired. I'm going to sleep in your bed, Papa Bear. I bet it's the most comfortable.' She weaves over the thick carpet like a drunkard and disappears into his room.

The air, to Suzanne, feels hilariously bright. The sun is a lion come to eat her. She wants to run out into it, travel to its centre.

'*Suzanne.*'

'*What?*'

'We've got to keep it together. Charity is sleeping. There might be danger. Edward.'

'I do have it together.'

'No, you don't. You're staring into the sun. You're going to burn out your retinas.' He grabs her shoulders and guides her to the floor; she sits cross-legged, her head in her hands.

'It's the dose, isn't it. It's the withdrawal.'

'I think so, yes.'

'What will it be like?'

'I don't know. A lot of things will rush back in. It will be a little, uh, overwhelming. Dreams. At night.'

'I already dream.'

'I told you that's not possible.'

'And this is?' she says, gesturing to the curved horizons, the invisible city, burning.

'This has always been possible. This was waiting for us.'

Suzanne rubs the sight back into her eyes and looks around for James. His face is slewed towards her; his mouth strains.

'Look! He's trying to say something.' Suzanne cradles his head, cups his face, feeling his cheekbones, still the brittle curved bones of a haemophiliac prince.

James struggles in her arms.

'Fssh,' he says.

'His fish.' Aquila goes to his room, but comes back empty-handed. 'We can't let him see them. Sludge.'

James kicks and mewls.

'He can hear you!' she says furiously.

'I'm sorry! I didn't . . . I thought he was unconscious. Or something.'

'James,' she says, with elaborate tenderness, 'they're gone. But you know what? Maybe there are more fish out there. In the great, rolling water. Or a cat. A cat for your shoulder.' She holds him, crooning, and he stills. His face is slick with tears and spit.

'And maybe the birds will come. Will come, and stay.'

She whispers it, close to his ear so Aquila can't hear. James's eyes fix on her for a moment, then veer away.

'Should we get him off the floor? Out of the sun?'

Neither of them wants to move too far from Charity. They end up camping just outside Aquila's room in a nest of coverlets, James between them.

'Remember when Charity was little and she used to play pirate?' says Aquila. 'She'd drag the blanket off her bed and put it on the carpet and that was her boat. She'd cry if you made her step off it, if her foot even touched the carpet. She'd say you were trying to drown her.'

'Yes,' says Suzanne, surprised. 'I do remember.' She watches, fascinated, Aquila's long fingers stroking James's hair. It makes her want to curl up like a seed in the earth and sleep, sleep, until the spring wakes her.

'What's that,' Aquila hisses. He pulls James against his body.

'What?'

'Listen.'

Suzanne thinks she knows what that sound is, that she's heard it long ago. It's the sound of glass breaking, but softly, glass efficiently and professionally broken with a blanket and a tap of the fist.

'Wake Charity,' she breathes. 'Give me James.'

And Aquila, for once in his life, does what she says.

She sits, straight-backed, with James across her lap. He weighs so little, this son of hers, like twigs she has collected.

Shadows fall across the white hallway and that is

how she sees them first, as sharp shadows cast by the climbing sun: Ezekiel with his stethoscope dangling, the stooped height of Piotr, Fen's pregnant belly.

'Welcome,' she says, and the shadows stop instantly, and stay so still, flat and innocent on the wall, that for a moment she thinks she has imagined them; that it's a confusion of her upper cortex. She is going mad, she thinks, mad from the lack of dose.

But then Ezekiel steps around the corner and throws a knife into the wall beside her head, and she knows this is real.

13

Aquila is moving slowly, trying to wake Charity without sound, but at the thunk of the knife on the wall he finds himself facedown on the bed with her knee in his back before he knows what's happening.

'Charity,' he squeezes out, 'it's me,' but she's already off him and at the door, moving sidelong, naked (he looks awkwardly away), scoping, like the trained panther she is.

Before he's even off the bed she is out in the hall. There's a confused cacophony, male shouts, then silence.

He comes upon a tableau: his daughter, haughtily nude, her foot on the neck of one man, the other at the point of her knife, a pregnant woman on her knees, his wife clutching James.

'Who are you?' the woman asks him, giving him a dour look from under her lashes.

'Why are you asking questions?' spits Charity. She steps harder on the man's neck.

There is a small, forced sound of pain.

'Charity,' he says at the same time as Suzanne.

The man at the point of the knife snickers a little, holding his jaw high to escape the blade.

Aquila says slowly, 'This is my daughter, Charity. My wife, Suzanne. My son . . .'

'Quiet,' hisses Charity, pressing the blade closer. 'Let me handle this.'

'This is my house,' says Aquila. He sits down. 'My son, James. I am Aquila.'

'Ezekiel,' says the man, and he runs his face lovingly down the blade. 'Surgeon at large.'

There is a taut silence.

'Aren't you going to introduce yourself, *frères*?'

'When she gets off my neck,' gasps the man under Charity's foot; she steps harder.

'Fen,' says the woman, closing her eyes. 'Fenella.'

'Charity,' says Aquila. 'Please.' He tries to make his breath even.

She looks at him for a moment, then rolls her eyes and steps off the man's neck. He groans and lurches onto his side, clutching the base of his skull. Charity kicks him lightly in the ribs. 'Get up.'

He springs to his feet, surprisingly fast for someone so tall, someone who looks so old. 'Piotr,' he says, rubbing his throat.

Charity, apparently unconcerned by her nudity, takes a small nick out of the surgeon's face and steps back, smirking. 'Why are you here?' she says to him.

'To sing to dry bones.'

'No bones here. Why are you in my father's house?'

'To look at its many rooms.' Ezekiel spits on his fingers, rubs the blood from his cheek.

'You're thieves, then.'

'Please! Charlatans.'

'Murderers. You threw a knife at my mother.'

'I've never murdered a soul. What, you think I missed her? And me, trained on the Carousel Wire?'

'What's wrong with your son?' says the woman, Fen, smoothing her belly. 'Why's he all twisted up?'

'He has palsy,' says Suzanne coldly.

'You came from outside,' says Aquila. 'How long have you been breathing the air?'

The three of them exchange amused glances. 'All our lives,' says Fen.

'Why are you not dead?' says Charity.

'We're not such poor creatures,' says Piotr. 'Not like you goldfish, under your glass.'

'You are human?' says Charity.

'How defined?' says Ezekiel, inclining his head.

'Don't fence with me: human. You were born from a woman? You breathe, beat? Eat, shit, bleed? Sleep? You have any wires?'

'I dance on wires. The question you've forgotten: do I dream?'

Suzanne's head is weaving, as if to an invisible tune. 'Edward dreamed,' she says.

'Where is this Edward?' says Piotr, his hand at his belt.

Charity, with a motion as fluid and beautiful as the holographic ballerinas who dance on the parapets at the Mariinsky Bar, kicks his hand into the air.

'Edward, he's dying from his wounds out there on the basalt. You know why? Because he messed with me. Now all of you mutts, be real clear with your hands.'

Piotr guffaws. 'So this is your daughter?' he says to Aquila. 'It's like the old saying, no? "May you be cursed with daughters."'

'Shut up, Piotr,' says Fen. 'She's dangerous.'

Charity smiles in evident delight, flexing her back from side to side. Her sleek, menacing body is so honed and armoured that even naked, she looks clothed. Edward's bite is lurid on her shoulder. 'You still haven't answered my question. What are you doing here?'

'They broke a window,' says Suzanne, lifting hazy eyes. 'There is air coming in.'

'Poor goldfish.' Piotr makes gulping faces.

James stirs.

'We were curious,' says Ezekiel. 'We're curious as otters, us. We've never got a look inside your houses before. What's it like in an aquarium, we wondered? What nectars do they eat? What silken sheets enfold them as they sleep their blank-slate dreams?'

'You're thieves,' says Charity. 'Looters.'

'Nothing here to loot.' Piotr indicates the walls, which are beginning to ooze and drip. 'Your playhouse is about to melt around your ears. Or don't you know even that?'

Aquila wonders if they can see what he can: the

signs of exhaustion under Charity's bravado. Her pupils are wandering slightly, her hands trembling. The bite on her shoulder is weeping.

They can't rely on her for much longer. He has to make them safe.

'Gentlemen,' he says, and gets to his feet. Piotr lifts his chin.

'Slowly, *druk*.'

'Gentlemen,' Aquila repeats. 'My liquor cabinet is about to unform. Will you join me in a last potation? I assume,' and he performs for Fen his most chivalrous bow, 'that you will not be partaking.'

The three of them look at each other. Piotr and Ezekiel laugh, shaking their heads.

'Piotr, *druk*, you want some vapour juice? Myself, I'd like to taste it. Shall we linger? A last supper?'

'Why not?'

'Fenella? Does the little one want some vapour juice?'

She shrugs irritably, cupping her belly. 'Can't hurt him. S'all thin air.'

'Not quite, *podruga*. It's molecules in a pattern, just like you. Only difference is, you hold yourself together, whereas their playhouse needs juice from the outside. From their grid.'

'If you'll allow,' Aquila says, using his most measured tones, 'I'll go and get the drinks. We have vodka, whiskey, a slivovitz infused with rose petals. Tonics, Tahitian limes.'

Ezekiel roars with laughter. '"And they on

honey-dews were fed, and drunk the milk of Paradise."
We have stumbled across it, no, Piotr? Go with him.'

'No,' says Charity. 'You will all stay here.'

'I'm afraid not, *dolcezza*. Who knows what he has hidden away back there? A replicated bullet still hurts quite a bit, *hena*?'

'He wants to get you a drink. Why, I don't know. But you'll sit back like good little urchins and say thank you nicely when he does.'

Ezekiel shakes his head, his smile becoming dangerous.

'I think it's time I took my knife back.'

'You can try.' Charity throws the knife into the air, spinning, and catches it so quickly that it's in her hand again before Aquila has properly registered what she's done.

'Yes, you have a great many pretty tricks. One day you must show me them all,' Ezekiel says, and then Aquila's vision, clouding and clearing like a kaleidoscope, betrays him: there is a series of complex blurs, and when he can see again all three of them have her on the ground, Fen struggling with her thrashing legs, Ezekiel with the knife at her throat, Piotr kneeling on her torn shoulder.

Suzanne and Charity are both screaming, and something in him has time to pause, savouring the way the screams form a harmonious pattern, Charity's an octave higher, like song.

He stumbles, slides down the wall. Time is lurching. A second unfolds its wings and balances on his hand, quivering. A minute passes with a beat of his hysterical heart.

Will he die, here and now?

But he doesn't die, and so must act. He wills himself to rise.

'Get off her, Piotr,' Ezekiel is saying, struggling to hold Charity's head.

'Are you mad? You can't hold her.'

'Get off her wound!' Ezekiel barks. Muttering, the older man shifts so that his knee pins the crook of her arm instead of her shoulder.

Fen plumps herself viciously on Charity's ankles.

'Christos, she fights,' says Ezekiel. 'Fen, get my bag.'

Fen scampers down the hall: she returns with a leather pouch just as Charity knees Piotr in the back of the head. He swears, and says to Ezekiel, 'Cut her.'

'Not necessary.'

'She doesn't believe that you will cut her. That's why she fights.'

'I won't cut her. There is no need. Fen, the dorm-wort. Hold her mouth.'

Charity's leg, heading again for Piotr's head, goes limp in mid-air and falls.

They climb off her, warily releasing their grasp. Charity lies still.

'Oh God.' Aquila's voice grates in his throat. 'What have you done to her?'

'Nothing. Sedative. I needed' – Ezekiel smiles like a lunatic – 'for her to calm down a little.'

Suzanne is bent over James like a broken puppet, rocking.

'Piotr. Go with Aquila to get these drinks of his. Quickly, *druk*, before it all unforms!'

Piotr walks towards Aquila; he sees each detail on his torn, heavily tasselled boots. He is hauled to his feet.

'Liquor,' says Piotr.

'Wait.' He struggles down to his knees beside Charity, turning her face, peeling back a lid, but there is nothing. White.

Ezekiel's hand closes warm over his own, pushing his fingers underneath her jaw. He feels the tom-tom of her pulse, and can breathe again.

'Get the drinks, *gospodin*. Your daughter is under my care.'

Fen thrusts the coverlet under Ezekiel's nose and he lays it over Charity's sprawled body, on which bruises are starting to appear, livid streaks under her breasts, on her legs.

'She's had quite some fight. Before we even got here. Yes?' Ezekiel's eyes, a brilliant, mesmeric blue, hold Aquila's.

'Yes. She's tired. Or you would never have taken her.'

'Let her sleep, then, yes?'

Piotr shadows Aquila down the hall, a hand on his shoulder. 'I'm not as nice as my *frère*,' he mutters into his ear. 'I'm no doctor. I've taken no oath. You understand me?'

'I understand. Look at me. You're not a doctor, but you can see, surely. I'm coming off a lifetime of dose. I'm nothing. I couldn't even save my daughter.' Stupidly, wretchedly, he is crying.

Piotr clicks his tongue. 'Be a man, *herr*.'

The house is crazily, liquidly unravelling. Piotr runs a hand down a dripping wall and sniffs it. The air is thick with chemical. Aquila tries not to breathe. The waterfall has solidified, glazing the edges of the steps. The arches of the doorways are hung with reeking stalactites. They duck under them and into the den. Aquila stoops to open the cabinet, but Piotr is too quick for him.

'Slowly, *gospodin*,' he breathes, seizing Aquila's wrist. 'Stand well back from it, so that I can see.'

Irritably, Aquila does what he says, drawing out bottles of white spirit and tonic from the lacquered cabinet, then scooping limes onto a tray.

'Can you help me? I can't carry it all.'

'Alright, alright.'

Piotr tucks a bottle of Veneshnya under his arm.

'Hurry. The door.' They scuttle under the archway as a thick glob detaches, falling on the carpet with a wet sizzle. This eastern part of the house is deteriorating more quickly than the others, deliquescing like stinking ice.

'Time to leave soon. Yes, *herr*?'

Aquila slows at the door of the music room; the harp is playing itself, the drops from the dissolving frame falling on the strings. He remembers, from his childhood, the sound of rain.

'Quickly.' Piotr examines the vodka under his arm.

When they get back, Ezekiel is talking in a low voice to James, feeling his shins. Aquila compresses his lips.

'Suzanne? What is going on?'

'I don't know,' she says. She is leaning against the walls, her eyes closed.

'I will tell you,' says Ezekiel, chafing James's feet. 'Your daughter is sleeping with my sedative. Your wife is in withdrawal from massive doses of hippocamp-ers. You are on something different, I'm not quite sure what, but it's wearing off. You're in some amount of cardiovascular distress. Your son has grade-four palsy, and is trying to say something I can't quite catch. His legs are cramping and I am rubbing them. Shall we have that drink?'

'Hurry up, would you?' Fen growls. She is sitting against the wall, her legs out in front of her, smoking some kind of ragged cheroot. The carpet is damp, slick. Viscous beads run down the wall like sweat.

Aquila fixes the drinks and hands one to Ezekiel. His sight is fracturing, turning into a radiant wheel, and he has to shake his head to clear his vision. It takes him a while to realise that James is restless, snuffling, beating his feet on the floor in a lopsided rhythm. Ezekiel holds up the figurine of the man with the cat.

'I found that in your son's hand.'

'Give it to him. Give it back. That's what he's trying to say.'

James moans.

'It's alright, pippin,' Ezekiel says, holding it close to his eyes. 'You'll have it back. I'm just a little interested in where you got it.'

Piotr leans in to peer at it.

'That's not him. It's never him.'

'It is.'

Fen looks up.

'So? Where did he get it?' Ezekiel waves the figurine slowly at Aquila, as if trying to hypnotise him.

'My daughter gave it to him. She got it in the Old Quarter. He liked the cat. Give it to him – now.' Aquila feels such a rush of fury along his limbs, sitting hot in his chest, that he thinks he will keel over.

'Softly, now.' Ezekiel puts the figurine into James's hand; the boy accepts it and is quiet. Ezekiel checks Charity, who is snoring painfully. He brings a torch from his pocket to shine in her eye, then lets her lid fall and sips at his drink. 'Lime. Tahitian lime. I've never had it before. Delicious little illusion, isn't it? Tart.'

'Hurry, *frère*,' murmurs Fen.

'Indeed. *Juveli*, all. To life.' Ezekiel knocks back his drink. 'Now,' he says, wiping a hand over his rough-shaven chin, 'we must act. Aquila, you and your family must leave here. It's agreed?' As if to illustrate his point, a section of the wall slides, sighing, to the ground, exposing the searing sky.

'We were going to take our chances.'

'And here we are. Your chances.' Ezekiel spreads his arms and smiles winningly. 'We move fast, us. You'll have to keep up. These are mule lassitudes, dead air. Not good, even for us. No lingering, sir.'

'How do you propose we keep up?' Aquila gestures to the slumped Suzanne, the stricken child in her arms, the prone Charity.

Ezekiel rummages in his leather pouch. 'For you, minkstocking, to strengthen the heart; for your wife, to bring her off the hippocampers, a touch of easy-Lethe. Just half a cap, to take the edge off. Your son, we'll have to carry him. Piotr? Could you, *druk*? And as for Sleeping Beauty here, I'll undertake to transport her myself.'

'Transport her where?'

'Away from here,' says Fen. 'Do you need to know where?'

'Certainly I do.' Aquila bends to Suzanne, pushing back her hair, but her face is erased, her eyes staring. She is a mannequin. 'Of course I do,' he says, feeling every capillary in his body as a small, iron thread of ache. 'You could be taking us anywhere. You could have any use in mind for us. We could prefer you left us here to rot with the house. We could prefer you kill us now.'

'Nobody is going to kill anyone,' says Ezekiel. 'We are taking you, Aquila, to the Eyries, to our home. Of course you can refuse to come. You can lie under that melting harp of yours and be part of this carrion symphony. You can hold your wife until you are bone. But I'm taking your daughter. And I'm taking your son.'

He holds out to Aquila a small pill, a speck of ebony in his hand.

'Why should I trust you?'

'Because you are dead already.'

Aquila hesitates, then holds out his hand.

'Good. And should you need another reason,'

Ezekiel tips the tiny dose into his palm, 'I have drunk a dram in your house. I can no more kill you now than I can my knocked-up sister here.'

'Sister?' says Aquila, swallowing the pill. The ache of his vessels ebbs. His vision clears. He looks from Fen, sandy-fair, ursine, her face heavy-boned and heavy-lipped, to the surgeon with his mercurial eyes and dark-stubbled jaw.

'In a manner of speaking,' says Ezekiel.

'Give my wife the dose. The one to take the edge off. Then let her decide for herself.'

'That's fair.' Ezekiel kneels, bites the cap in two, squeezes Suzanne's jaw open and puts the dose under her tongue. He massages her throat. Her eyes slowly uncloud, like a phone lens with a call coming through.

'Suzanne,' Aquila says. 'They want to take us to where they live. Do you want to go? Or stay?'

'It's a little late,' she says, 'for you to divorce me.'

'Then we'll go,' he says. His body feels resurgent, young. He pulls her to her feet and against him, tucking her underneath his chin, her head on his chest. He feels the way they fit, familiar, as if they held each other yesterday instead of years ago.

When they break from each other, he's not sure how much time has passed. Ezekiel has taken the dissolving rags of the coverlet from Charity's body and is using them to rub down James, taking the remnants of the bright clothes from his back. Piotr lifts him to his back and secures him inside the tattered fur of his hood. The boy looks out with frightened eyes.

'Let's go.' Ezekiel lifts Charity in his arms, fitting her head to his shoulder. Fen swears as one of the phone lenses rolls stickily from the wall, just missing her.

'Out. Now,' commands Ezekiel. All three of them pull a tassel at their waist. Their boots sprout blades and they skim down the hall, towards the shivering fish-eye of the feature window.

'Follow,' Ezekiel calls back over his shoulder. 'Run. Run!'

As they pass the bathroom, Aquila pauses to see the clammy remains of *Hive* slop into the bath. It's still the same green, and he treasures for one moment the faint echo of a vast and luminous calm he will never know again.

14

Charity wakes in waves. Long surges push her flat against a strong moving body.

'Edward,' she says.

She wakes a little more, brings her teeth together on fur. 'Edward,' but then she remembers, and tells her hand 'windpipe', which should do the trick, but all it gets her is a burning wrist, a sharp lurch and an angry voice saying, 'Be still, can't you? I'm skating, if you hadn't noticed.'

There is a wind in her face like she's never felt, spicy and cool, feeding her. Her lungs suck at it.

'Whoa,' says the voice, 'whoa, *frères*,' and the surging and the warm fur cushioning her head and the stream of spiced wind stops.

She makes a small, bitter sound of complaint.

'What is it now?'

'She's waking. I have to rearrange her, if she's going to thrash about.'

'Drug her again.'

'I can't do that, Fen. The dose I gave her was dangerous already. I'll not risk it.'

'Charity!'

'Stand back, the both of you. If she hears familiar voices she'll wake faster.'

'Is she alright?'

'*Back.*'

'How much longer do we have to carry them?'

'Until we get out of the Golem Plains. Or when night falls and the ground cools. Whichever is first.'

'My bloody back hurts.'

'I'm sorry for it, *podruga*. But you have the lightest load. We must bring in the cargo. Were you born a kite? Raised a kite?'

'I'm seven months gone.'

'Were you born a kite? Raised?'

'Yes. Were you?'

'No. There you have me! So, shall we? *'Avanti, frères. Challo!'*

The wind starts again. Charity takes long draughts that set her heart beating at a higher frequency, that turn the clock spring of her nervous system widdershins.

Warm. Warm fur. She is drifting again.

Something is troubling her, way down in the old familiar pit of her being, the wise reptile part of her that says 'windpipe!' but she's too sleepy and dazed and wet between the legs to care.

Warm. Fur.

Edward, she says, and just for an instant she's back in her bed, in her suite at the top of the Skyworthy Building, the training day over, her sleeping hood on, curled into Edward's belly; but why is there wind, how did this wild rushing wind get into her tight-sealed room? And then she is not in her bed, there is nothing beneath her, she is falling and falling, until she is nothing at all.

—

'Charity. Come on.'

It feels like she's facedown in feathers, suffocating.

'Charity. Charity! Come on, *mädchen*. Wake.'

She opens her eyes a misty crack. A burning seam of light, a dark blur. She pulls herself together with everything she's got.

What are you?

Bounter.

What does that mean?

I win.

She focuses. Her eyes flinch, agonised jelly. She focuses again.

His back is turned to her.

Spine.

He turns to meet her leap, takes the brunt of it on his chest, grunts, and falls against the window, his head framed in light.

She breathes into his mouth, and to her own amazement, spares him.

He springs to the balls of his feet, overbalancing the two of them with perfect judgement so that they land back on the bed, his hand under her skull, cushioning it.

'So, you're awake.'

'Half awake,' she says.

'Gods of stricken rock, I'd hate to see you at full strength. Or love to, maybe.'

She touches the stethoscope around his neck. 'Why do you wear this?'

'Doctor's necklace. Reads hearts.'

'I know what it is. You're really a surgeon?'

'And apothecary. At large.'

His weight is still on her.

'What is this place?'

'The Eyries. In a minute, you can look out the window. Then you'll see.'

'In a minute?'

'Yes.'

His mouth is close to hers. She draws aside his fur jerkin, baring a dark-furred nipple, touching it with her thumb. His chest warmly beats. He is human.

He licks her lips. 'Salt. You need water. And I have to clean up that wound.' He slides off her and she hears the sound of water poured from a jug, which wakens a mad thirst.

'Here.' He holds her head. She drinks frantically. The water is cool, and tastes green somehow.

'Rainwater. Careful now, that's enough.'

'Rain?'

'Perhaps your *dedushka* told you about it. Water from the sky.'

'I know what rain is. There's no dome here, nothing at all?'

'Rock. And above it sky. You don't want to spend too much time out on the plateau, especially with the wind in the wrong direction, but it's not too bad in the Eyries, because of the height. The air is clean up here. Can you stand up?'

He helps her to the window, a large rough square cut into the rock. She leans on the deep sill and looks out.

They are so high up that there's no ground, only blue, limitless reaches of air above a blanket of cloud. The sun here is truly a star, white and burning.

She watches, fascinated, the creatures that swim through the blue haze.

'Birds. You've never seen them?'

She shakes her head. 'Pictures.'

He leans out and whistles, and one of the creatures comes straight for her. She throws a hand up, crying out.

'Don't be afraid. Look.'

The thing perches on his wrist, teetering. It's black, sleek, smug; it regards her with a supercilious eye.

'This is a crow. They hunt for us.'

'Can I touch it?'

'If it will let you. Careful.'

She strokes, with one finger, the bird's oily breast. It looks down at her hand and catches her finger in its beak. She gasps, but it's gentle: it gnaws a little at her then shakes itself and flies back into the endless sky.

She wants only to look and look at that sky, but Ezekiel makes her lie down again. 'Rest.'

The room has hardly any furniture, just the bed – wooden, painted wildly and brightly with flowers and cats and birds, heaped with furs – a table with the jug and a wooden bowl, a trunk. He soaks a cloth and leans over her, cleaning the wound.

She ignores the pain by looking at his face. Hypnotist's eyes. What was it he said? Charlatan. His mouth seems to be laughing even when it's still.

'Is this your room?'

'Yes.'

'Will you keep me here?'

'For now. He'll want to see you.'

'Who is this He?'

'You don't know? You bought that toy. The one James has.'

'The figurine? I bought it in the Old Quarter.'

'They didn't tell you his name?' He takes a heavy, pungent grease from the bowl and smears it over her shoulder, sealing the wound.

She gasps. 'No. The old man who sold it to me said he was a pirate.'

'An iron pirate. He rode the trains, in the old days. His name is Gid Narwhal.'

The crows cry knowingly outside.

'And who is he to you?'

Ezekiel hesitates; grins. 'Our father.'

'Literally?'

'No.'

'When will I meet him?'

'When you're well.'

'When will that be?'

'When I say. Not yet.' He puts his hand on her belly, warming her all through. 'What was the thing that bit you?'

'A delusion.'

He traces the line of the bruising around her midriff. 'These seem pretty real to me.'

As he nears her breast her breath deepens; her broken ribs sing in unison. She curls a hand around his neck and brings him down to her, so that their chests meet, bared and beating.

Over his shoulder the blue window sails in her vision, thick with the black-beaked birds.

15

He is trapped now in his head. He is a doll, to be hefted on a back, to be passed from hand to hand. His limbs ache steadily. His thick tongue stumbles.

And this, all along, was what he was.

He thinks of his fish, bright sludge in a melted bowl.

The tears run into his ears, and he can't stop even that.

These people, the kites, are not unkind: they bring him thick soup and feed him patiently. One woman reads him a book about a cat that eats meringues. What are meringues? He can't ask her.

They watch him, waiting for him to dream.

'I already dream. I've dreamed for years,' he shouts, but the breath barely stirs his lips.

He falls into restless sleep, and sees Edward on the stairs of the studio. Below them, the wooden ape, sticks piercing its neck, lets out a howl and wind takes the house, blowing it into smoking fragments that circle like birds. Edward turns to James, pointing down at the ape. He comes close to whisper. 'Unmade,' he says. 'Unmade.'

Faces loom over him. He is sat up, laid down.

Each person who moves him takes the figurine from him, holds it to the light from the window, examining it, then returns it without comment to his shaking hand. His heart gallops with fury each time.

The morning after their arrival at the Eyries, he wakes with a cat sitting on the end of his bed. He makes his strongest effort yet to move: he feels as if he bursts small capillaries in his head. Nothing happens. But the cat, a tigerish fellow with an ear half gone and a luxuriant cravat of cream fur, stretches first one and then the other ginger-britched hind leg, walks up James's body and stands on his chest.

James can't breathe. The cat is huge; its paws grip his brittle sternum, and he gasps. It lowers its head and presses a cool pink nose against his.

'Hello,' James says. Does he say it? Do his lips move?

The cat jumps off his chest, curls in the space between his arm and his ribs, and vibrates itself. It actually makes its own thrumming music. His heart beats in time to the languorous rhythm. The cat's warmth floods the frail glass of him.

It's like when he could sing.

He feels like a squillionaire.

When the woman comes to give him his soup, she laughs and scritches the cat under the chin, making the vibration switch into overdrive as it plunges its claws into the blankets.

'Treacle likes you then, eh? Do you miss your cat at home, scrap?'

She pushes his hair back from his forehead.

Cat at home? Are cats so commonplace to them? Are they all squillionaires?

The ginger tom is only the first of the cats who prowl into his room, spring with their dancers' feet onto his bed, nose under his elbows, curl in the crook of his legs, toy with the fringe of his bedclothes, bat and lick and snarl at each other, purr him home from his dreams. It becomes a joke with the women who nurse him.

'She won't even sleep with me anymore,' says Robin, picking up a fat calico by the scruff and mock-shaking her. 'He's got them all enchanted.'

'It's good company for him,' says the placid Grace, chafing his feet. 'God knows his parents are in no fit state . . .'

'He can hear you, you know. Ezekiel says.'

'Ezekiel says. I don't know. There's nobody home if you ask me.'

Nobody home, nobody home. He leaves his body increasingly. In dream, in reverie, when the light comes low through the window in the afternoon, when everyone else is sleeping. The skin between dreaming and waking becomes a little thinner every day, rubbed, easy to burst. Sometimes he thinks the only thing that keeps him from vanishing right out of the window and becoming another layer of sky is the weight of cats on his bed.

In his dreams he can walk just fine. Sing, and draw. What he misses most is the drawing. His harness, precious harness, gone to mush.

On the third day Grace dresses him. Up until now he has lain naked, like a baby. When he came in they scrubbed the lurid stains of his old clothes off him and swaddled him in furs. It's cold in the Eyries when the sun moves from the windows: fires burn in the grates. Grace lifts him easily into her arms and puts him on the hearth, and dresses him in rough cream linens, a loose shirt, trousers. Last she puts the figurine back in his palm and closes his fingers on it.

He thinks she will maybe take him to see Aquila and Suzanne, but she takes him along a steep hallway that leads up and up through the centre of the Eyries like a bent spine. The stone floor is so worn that she slips every now and then, and swears.

The door at the end of the hallway is carved with fish. Grace tucks him over her shoulder and pulls at a long scarlet cord. Somewhere a deep bell clangs.

The door opens a crack.

'Well?'

'The boy is here to see him. The goldfish boy.'

The door swings wider, and James, with an effort, focuses his crossed eyes. He can see only dark red velvet. It brushes against his cheek.

'Leave him. Put him down.'

Grace places him on the floor and backs away. The door swings to behind her, causing the red curtains to billow.

'Boy for you. Boy you asked for.'

'Bring him.'

A tall, brawny man plucks him off the ground. He smells of animal fat, musk. His long beard tickles James's face.

'Bring him here. Closer. Put him on the bed.'

The room is dim. James squints to see. Candles gutter in the corners. He can see nothing but a towering bed with curtains of the same red velvet. The man's meaty hand seizes the edge of them and pulls them aside.

'Not much of a boy, but here it is.' He dumps James on the coverlet. The velvet of it is stitched with patterns, fish leaping from waves. A whirlpool sucks at a tilting ship. The dust makes him sneeze.

An old man is leaning against a mountain of pillows. James has never seen such an old man. His face has disappeared into itself: the eyes are sunk in hollows like animals looking out from caves. He wears a red cap heavily embroidered with gold. His nose sprouts white hair.

'Closer.'

The bearded man sighs, lifts James, drops him at the old man's elbow.

'Very well. That's all.'

The curtain falls. They are alone in a musty darkness.

James can hear the old man breathing, like someone sawing wood. He whimpers.

'You're afraid, eh? No need. Won't eat you, little

stick like you. Not worth putting my teeth in for, *accha*?'

James jumps and shudders as the old man's hand grabs his shin.

'Twisted up, en't yeh? Ezekiel was right then. Palsy.'

The hands explore him coolly, following the kinks of his crooked limbs, lifting his jaw to feel his throat, burrowing in his hair.

'Still got a brain in there, don't yer? You understand me well enough.' His hands close on the bent claws of James's hands.

'I hear tell you had this.' He takes the figurine. James makes a scratchy sound of protest.

'No need to fret yerself. You'll have it back. I wanted to feel if they had the cat. They do. They have that right. It's me, you know that? Back when I was young, stalking around on the roofs of the trains with me hook and a whip and a knife. The cat was Martello. Portuguese, the beast. Rogue of a thing. Smart as lightning.'

There is a mew in the darkness. The old man hawks out a laugh. 'Jealous, are yeh? Come out of your hole, then, meet my guest. I hear tell,' he says to James, 'that the Eyries cats like you.'

The invisible cat sits on James's rucked-up foot, kneading the coverlet with a brisk snagging sound.

'I always trust a man cats like. One other thing. I hear tell you talk in your sleep. No one can know what you're saying, of course. Tongue like yours won't make words. But the women say you're travelling. They can tell by the look of yeh.'

He takes James's hands in his.

'Don't know what you're meant to be doing with these. But it's something. Oh yes, something. They have a calling.' He thrusts the figurine back into James's palm.

'So, someone still remembered me. Down there in your aquarium. All busted up now, I hear. Poor fish.' James's eyes are accustoming themselves to the dark: he can see the old man tracing the glittering fish on the bed.

'I never saw the sea, you know. But my family were pirates, ship pirates. The Narwhals live on their wits, boy. But now my wits are going. Yeh, I'm on my way out. These kites will have to get by on their own.'

He presses James's forehead with his palm, causing a giddy rush. James blinks.

'Micah! Come here, yeh felon.'

The bearded man hurls back the curtain. 'What?'

'Take this boy back to the infirmary. Tell them I'll want to see him tomorrow.'

Micah picks him up by the scruff.

'Life's not so bad,' the old man tells James, 'when you can travel.'

He falls back onto the pillows, curls his hand over the cat and closes his eyes.

Micah lets the curtain fall.

16

Dreams turn Aquila's hair white.

He loses track of the days. Sometimes it seems they are still on that terrible journey, clinging to the backs of the skating kites: the endless rock, the glare. When they first came to the Eyries, their backs, left naked as their clothes dissolved, were blistered raw from the sun. They were laid on their fronts, and he felt like he fell miles and years, through the bed and the height of the rock and the very earth itself, the battered, indifferent earth, down to its core of fire.

The dreams ride him and ride him. Perch on his back and seep through him.

Suzanne, in the bed next to him, cries out sometimes. He remembers what he said to her in the hallway of the melting house, that it might be 'overwhelming', and sniggers a little.

Yeah. Might be.

All the dreams he hasn't had storm through him. And memories. Rain caught in his fat infant palm. A crayon picture, a house and sun. Strapped to his father's back, in a running crowd. Marrying Suzanne in a roadside temple. Making *Spannerworks*, the piece that got him noticed. The first time on the ceiling wires, at art school, spinning helplessly. But what he dreams of most of all is the wooden ape in the dark basement, snarling at nothing, slowly coming undone.

One morning he wakes to find Suzanne facing him, her eyes open.

'I miss the dose,' she says. She rolls over.

After a few days, they stop giving them the sleeping draughts. One morning he finds he can sit up, look around. His back is shedding itself in long festoons: the bed is disgustingly full of dead skin.

'James,' says Suzanne.

'Where is he? And Charity?'

'I don't know. Here. Somewhere.'

He feels poured out. His hands shake.

'Your hair is all white. You look like an old man.'

'You don't look so crash-hot yourself.' He pulls himself from the bed.

'We've lost our children,' says Suzanne, yawning.

'It's sort of restful.'

He wraps a blanket around himself and teeters over to the window, leaning on the rock sill to look down. Sick, plunging vertigo. He clutches at the walls.

'There is *no ground*.'

'What do you mean? There must be ground.'

'Nothing. Only sky. We must be unimaginably high.'

'There were ropes. At the end. They brought us up in baskets, on ropes.'

'I don't remember that part.'

'I only remember bits.'

'But you remember the other things, before all that. James being born? Our wedding?'

'Yes.' They lean on the sill, looking out at the wheeling birds.

'I'd forgotten about them. The birds,' says Aquila.

'James used to see birds. Behind his eyes, he said. Sometimes I would see them too.'

'You were hallucinating. You were taking too much. That's why you lost it, in the house, at the end, became a kind of zombie.'

'We all lost it. You weren't exactly a model of –'

'I know. I know. I was useless. When Edward attacked Charity I did nothing. I'm an old man, Suzanne. Look at me.'

'Well, don't get maudlin. We made it.'

'Yes, whatever that means.'

'It means this. Another breath.'

'What, we stay here?'

'There isn't a choice, it seems.' They gaze into a distance that doesn't exist.

'The city may recover. We could go back.'

'Not for a long time.'

'But some day.'

'Let's just be alive, for now.'

He looks at her profile. She has her head tipped

back to the sun. Can it be that she's enjoying this?

'How do you feel? Without your dose?'

'Irritable, most of the time,' she says. 'Kind of – you know, as if everything's a bit sharp, a bit hard around the edges. I remember James being born, realising he was damaged. It hurts. But I remember other things, now. And I think it's not as hard for me, perhaps, as it is for you. I was getting a bit immune, at the end. Things were starting to bleed through. I could remember Fountain Street. The fish market, you know? The cobbler who spoke Hindi.'

'That's where we met. Isn't it?'

She turns to him, her eyes wide with amusement. 'You know, I don't know. I've told so many stories about it, and it was so long ago. I forget.'

'I remember the wedding,' he says. 'That temple at the end of the sweetmeat district. It was dark inside, smoky. It smelt of butter from the candles.'

'Temples. Are we that old?'

'Your cobbler put the red mark on your forehead. If it hadn't been for him, they would have chased you out of there. You were wearing next to nothing. As you liked to do.'

'But in the end,' says Suzanne, frowning, 'they put the flowers in my hair.'

'Red flowers. Hibiscus.'

'Yes.'

They experiment with looking at each other.

One of the kite women comes into the room, holding armfuls of clothes.

'Since you're feeling better, thought you might like to get dressed. Maybe come with me and see where you'll be working.'

'Working?' says Aquila uneasily.

'Yes. Of course yes. Even kings work here, dearie. While your legs and your lungs hold out, you'll work.'

'I'd like to see my son.'

'Can't. He's with him.'

'With who?'

'You'll meet him soon enough. He's getting to you, he says.'

He and Suzanne stand like children, and like children dress in the clothes brought to them, the clothes of kites: leggings, the heavy-tasselled mukluks, silk tunics, frogged jerkins.

The burns are healing, but his body still feels raw, rubbed by the unfamiliar fabric. He's glad there are no mirrors in the room. He would hate to catch sight of himself, dressed like this, white-headed. He can feel the seams in his face.

'Charity. What about our daughter?'

The kite throws back her head and laughs.

'Still playing doctor, I think you'll find. Ah well, they'll have to come out soon enough to eat. Come on. Come and see the kitchens.'

Reluctantly, they follow. *'Kitchens?'* he hisses.

'Will they teach us to make cake?'

'This is serious.'

'Oh come on. You have to savour the irony.'

'I thought that was sucked out in your last ass job?'

They bicker their way down the hall.

The kitchens are vast, room upon room of sullenly burning grates, kites in long aprons doggedly chopping and mixing, turning spits. One room is full of apples, stacked in haphazard piles. Suzanne takes one and squeezes.

'Look,' she says in wonder, giving it to Aquila. 'It's not a replication.' He presses it in his palm: it stays hard and crisp, no give of air.

'Can I taste it?' he asks the cook, who is cutting and coring apples with furious speed. He nods, barely looking up. And so they huddle in a corner of the room, by a guttering fire and a simmering pot fragrant with the stewing juice, and reacquaint themselves with paradise.

17

Charity's audience with Gid Narwhal, postponed while she and his surgeon devoured one another, takes place in the evening, as the windows hold the rare cobalt hue of mountain dusk. 'The hour,' Ezekiel calls it, 'of the wolf.'

They are delirious, weak, staggering a little into each other on the steep incline that leads to Narwhal's door.

'We forgot to eat,' says Ezekiel.

'No. We ate. At least once. Meat, real meat. Spiced. I remember it.'

'Oh yes. The bear meat.'

Charity is wearing a dress Ezekiel had fetched for her: the same blue as the dusk sky, with sleeves that brush the floor, the kind of velvet dress the kite women wear for special occasions.

'Is this a special occasion?' she'd asked him as he buttoned up the breast of it.

'Sort of.'

'You know, I still don't understand why I'm here. Why you thought he'd like me.'

'Because I do.'

'Do you always like the same things?'

'God, no.'

'Then?'

'He likes a curiosity, these days. At his End-of-Days. And he likes women, beautiful women. Though he's blind.'

'I'm a curiosity?'

'Indeed, you are,' he'd sighed. He'd rested his hands around her throat, on her chest. 'You need an amulet.'

'Why?'

'Everyone has one. For luck. To say who you are.'

'You don't have one.'

'I do and all,' he'd said, showing the stethoscope.

She'd put her palm over its cool metal disc. 'I don't want people to know who I am.'

'Why not?'

'Because I don't know, nowadays.'

'What were you? When you did know?'

'A bounter. An attack animal. Something chemical. A star.'

'I think I know who you are. A little.'

'Who?' She'd felt a faint unease, a memory stirring. *Remember to breathe.*

'Maybe the amulet will help you. I'll carve you one. And then you can say if you care to wear it.'

At the door, she presses against him, savouring his shape.

'Come. He'll be waiting.'

'Why are there fish on the door?'

'Crest of his family. The pirate Narwhals.'

Ezekiel pulls at the bell; the door is opened by the impassive Micah. He looks down from his six-and-a-half feet at Charity, his lip curling, and she's reminded for a moment of her opponents in the ring; her hackles rise.

'He asked for her,' Ezekiel says.

'Mebbe. Where you goin', then?' Micah flings out an arm to stop him following Charity into the room.

'With her.'

'Didn' ask for you.'

'He'll get me and like it.'

Micah sniffs, lets the red curtains fall over the archway, and wanders off down a dark passage, muttering 'Didn' ask. Didn' want.'

The dim room is as red as the inside of lids. In the kite style, there's not much in it but the enormous, elaborate bed, the curtains gathered at the top in the mouth of a sword-nosed fish.

'*Otyets,*' says Ezekiel.

The curtains part a little, held back with a spiral-carved stick.

'Well? You brought her?'

'She's here.'

'Come closer.'

The hem of Charity's dress drags on the ground, creating a wake of dust.

'Closer.'

Charity hesitates, feels Ezekiel's warmth at her back. She lifts her skirts and climbs onto the bed.

'Not you, sprig,' Narwhal tells his surgeon, and lets the curtain fall.

'Not a chance, old man,' Ezekiel says, catching at the curtain and pulling it aside.

'The light hurts my eyes.'

'Tripe. You're blind.'

'Doctors,' Narwhal sneers to Charity. 'So literal.'

Ezekiel grins and leans against the bedpost.

'Your name I know,' says Narwhal in Charity's direction. 'Your brother I know. Quite a talent, your brother.'

'He's sick.'

'In a manner of speaking.'

'He used to be able to draw. He inherited my father's talent.'

'I don't know anything about his drawings. He hasn't told me about them.'

'Can he talk?'

'Sounds. He makes sounds. He's quite eloquent. Maybe he'll talk one day, if he finds a use for it.'

'It wasn't supposed to happen, that a disease like his could get past the screenings. We all thought . . .'

'Thought?'

'That he was . . . normal.'

'What a dull thing to wish for.'

'He's sick. He's miserable.'

'At first. Now he's alright. You'll see him; you'll know.'

'Gid has a talent,' Ezekiel murmurs.

'As do we all. And you, *mädchen*? Come here.'

Charity flicks back her skirts and sits, just beyond the reach of his hand. He clicks his tongue, seizes her skirts and pulls, so that she falls forward, almost into his lap.

'Take it easy,' says Ezekiel.

'I'm a dying man, doctor, isn't it so? Had we but world enough and time, darlin' . . . but we don't. I'm an old tree. Toppling.'

Charity twitches her skirts out of Narwhal's hand.

'I don't think I'll wear this dress again,' she tells Ezekiel. 'There's too much advantage to the opponent.'

'Opponent, is it? You're mighty ready to fight, dear.'

'Gunslinger, she is,' says Ezekiel. 'Swashbuckler.'

'Failed artist,' she says. 'Trained dog.'

Narwhal's blind eyes meet hers without expression, but his face creases with amusement, and he holds out a hand. 'Gid Narwhal. Erstwhile iron pirate. Lifelong pickaroon.'

She takes the hand. Like something carved, then coated with rumpled silk. She fights revulsion: she has never seen anyone this old. He is mottled with age, rotten with it.

'What's a pickaroon?'

'A rogue, my peach. A wanderer. One who lives off his wits.' The coverlet heaves and a piebald cat emerges, opening its mouth to show the pink within, arching its supple back. Although the Eyries are overrun with cats, and Ezekiel's (a striped tom, Applehead) rides often on his shoulder and catches at their ankles in bed, she's not yet used to them. Their bodies amaze her: she's jealous of their flexibility, their ability to right themselves in the air. They make her want to fight again.

'Shank,' says Narwhal, indicating the cat, who puts its front paws on Charity's velvet leg and sniffs her over with evident disdain.

'He smells Applehead,' says Ezekiel.

She is not sure she likes being examined by this ancient and his patched beast.

'Am I your prisoner?' she asks Narwhal.

'Hardly. Seems you were more than a match for my outskaters. What do you think then, Ezekiel, could she take you? Could she make her escape?'

Ezekiel lounges against the bedpost. 'She has her tricks.'

Narwhal leers. 'I don't doubt it. The trouble is, trickster, gunslinger, that there's nowhere for you to go.'

'The city? Do you know what happened to it?'

'Not yet. I won't send anyone near it yet. It will be a calamity, that I know. It will fall into itself, eat itself. The air is bad. Few will survive. I saw it, last time. I know how it will go.'

Charity plays with Shank's ears. She thinks of the cloud bars, the sartoriums, the parlours, the bounter rings, the museums, her father's hallowed works sliding off the walls.

'It's a hell of a big world, just to disappear.'

'There's a hell of a big world disappears every time you wash your neck.'

'This is supposed to be some kind of consolation?'

'No. Just an observation. I'm not in the business of consoling.'

'What business are you in, then?'

'Business? I've given it up entirely. I'm a dying man, after all. Isn't that right, doctor?'

'If you say so.'

'I do say so. It's knacky. Everyone must do what you say, when you're dying.'

'As if they didn't always, old swindler.'

'Hark at him! There's gratitude, the wretch. I should have left him lying out there on the stones where I found him.'

'You're not from the Eyries?' says Charity, turning to Ezekiel.

'Not born. He found the infant me in the mule lassitudes. Imagine!'

'All alone?'

'Alone,' says Narwhal, 'and naked as the truth.'

'Who could have left you out there?'

'Flungouts, or the dead.' Narwhal chews on his tongue, remembering. 'I didn't enquire too closely as to his lineage, as the poor downless chick was blue. I scooped it up and took it to the good air. I found a corpse boy too, his brother maybe. This one wanted to live. I let it.'

Ezekiel bows his head, his hand on the old man's foot.

'How did you find this place?'

'Sight. Dreams. I led myself here, and whoever

would follow. Not many. Not many as would follow up a mountain like this on the say-so of a dream. But later more came. They heard about me. They found the way. There's enough now. As I believe I told you, sprig.'

'Are you sorry I brought her, then?'

'You're not sorry,' the old man says tartly. 'That's plain. You reek of her, did you know?'

'And she reeks of me, and we reek of each other. Does it make you nostalgic?'

'Puppy. When I was your age I was twice the rake.'

'You approve then?'

'Of her?' Narwhal turns his head, considering. His hand grasps at the air, finds her face. His fingers measure her.

'You've strong bones. Good strong bones. Not like your brother, there. He's a hollow reed. Wind sings through him. And yet, he endures.'

'He's the best of us. I've always said it.'

'And you? What are you best of?'

'The killers,' says Charity, tossing her head.

'Is that right? And what did you kill for, back in the dome?'

'Sport. Fame.'

'We don't kill for such things here. We don't have such luxuries. You were – what? An assassin? A huntress?'

'A gladiator.'

'There's corruption for you.'

'If you like. I was sent to the dojos at the age of seven. I was the cream. I perfected myself. Or rather, I was perfected. Built.'

'And what now will you build?' Narwhal's milky eyes seem to fix on her.

'I don't know.' The cat yawns and settles against her.

'Can you skate?'

'What? No.'

'Could be you'll learn. I need a new outskater. Fen will be laid up soon.'

'What do they do, these skaters? Besides breaking into houses.' She glares at Ezekiel, who has his knife out, whittling a nub of wood. She can smell the fragrance of it.

'They are my scouts. My scavengers. My border guards. My newshounds.'

'This whole roost does your bidding?'

'What else should it do? I built it. When I came here it was just a howling rock. I saw it whole and made it whole. And now the very birds of the air are its citizens.' He lifts his chin, and she sees for a moment the man he was, the man striding the roofs of the iron trains.

'What was it like, the world? Before the End-of-Days took it?'

He laughs. The rumble of it shakes his chest, and he coughs urgently. Ezekiel pauses in his whittling.

Narwhal wipes phlegm on the bright-stitched waves. 'Beautiful, filthy, cruel, like any world with humans in it. Full of wonders and downfalls. The kind of world that would have an End-of-Days. And then have it all over again. The kind of world that forgets all it knows over and over. Kind of like this one.'

'What happened? To the dome?'

'Who knows? Everything falls. This too, this tower of mine. Please Chance I'll be gone before.'

He sighs, his crumpled lids closing. His shirt has fallen open and she sees what lies on his chest: a bone on a plaited cord. Or a tooth perhaps, the tooth of some unimaginable beast.

Ezekiel shakes his foot lightly.

'I'll bring her again?'

Narwhal opens one eye. 'Yes, bring her again. Your trickster. I like the way she smells.'

The surgeon kneels on the bed, warming the stethoscope under his arm, then lifts the bone amulet delicately aside and presses the metal against the old man's chest. He listens.

'Still got a heart, then, have I?'

'And it beats, what's more. You'll live another day.'

'Close the curtains. The light.'

Ezekiel presses his face to Narwhal's grizzled cheek and steps off the bed. Charity lifts the protesting Shank off her skirts.

They draw the curtains and leave the room. She looks back once at the fish that holds the bed that holds the old man dreaming, the tooth from some deep-water creature on his chest.

18

James has his own amulet now, and all the women are talking because Gid Narwhal himself carved it.

It's a reindeer, one foot lifted proudly, a toadstool speared on its antlers.

'What does it mean?' Grace says, not quite touching it, resting her fingertips on James's collarbone.

'It's what the princes had, before,' Robin says. 'Deer, stags, they're for princes. That's what Micah says he said.'

'Quite the favourite, isn't he? This little princeling fish.'

They are not quite friendly.

'Is it time for the royal audience?'

'The daily meeting of minds.'

'What do they talk about?'

'They don't talk about anything, do they. Stands to reason.'

'I'm not so sure. He almost said something, this

morning. When I was bathing him. The water was too hot. He made a sound, but not just a sound. Almost like a word.'

'He's in there, is he? The surgeon was right.'

'Oh, he's in there, alright. Look at him watching us.'

'Anyway, it's time. Will you take him?'

'You.'

'I'm busy.'

'And I'm not?'

In the end Robin takes him, toiling up the slick stone of the hallway.

'You're getting a heavy princeling, en't you. The good meat he says you must have, the best butter, best of everything. Wonder what spell you've put on him? Without saying one word?'

James concentrates, keeps his eyes from crossing, and stares her down. The reindeer is heavy on his frail chest.

She falters, then kisses his head awkwardly. 'Well, no harm in you, I suppose.'

She leaves him at the door, gives it a sharp knock and is off before Micah opens it. The giant looks down at him. 'So they've brought the post. What kind of package is this?' He plucks him up by the scruff.

'Your fish,' he says, and drops him on the bed.

James has learnt to cherish the moment when the curtain falls on the dark, musty tent of Gid Narwhal's bed. The old man's breathing no longer scares him. Sometimes Narwhal will speak; sometimes he will open the door of silence, letting a larger room unfold, a room in which they are alone with their own breathing, the old man's bubbling in his chest, James's a wet effort, until the breathing becomes something else and the room expands once again, and they are somewhere else entirely, and he sees things.

Narwhal is teaching him. He speaks only sometimes.

After these sessions James finds he can move a little more, open his fingers, shape letters with his lips. One day he will say something. He practises. 'Gid.'

Narwhal arranges for him to have a cat of his own, a black kitten with white whiskers that she rubs against his face.

'Well-known fact that cats aid healing,' he tells James. 'Something to do with the frequency of the purr. M'surgeon swears by them. Hospital's full of 'em. You name her, now. She'll know her name, even if you don't say it.'

James names her Caribou, and she sleeps on his chest, purring like a hive full of bees. When he wakes in the night, gasping, from a dream of being fitted for a collar, she is there, blinking lazily, unconcerned.

Aquila and Suzanne come to see him every day. At first they are tearful, cling to him, but these days they're working so hard in the kitchens they don't seem to have much energy for all that. Aquila brings him morsels that he's made, cups of stew and soup, chunks of heavy breads and puddings. Suzanne is breezy, wears her hair tied back; it doesn't tickle his face as it used to. Her hands are blackened from stoking the fires. She leaves a grimy thumbprint near his jaw when she leans over to kiss him. They ask him about Narwhal, who is still yet to 'get to them'.

'What does he want with you? What does he say to you?' But he's not obliged to answer questions, these days.

Charity comes more rarely. She is training, she tells him, learning to skate and walk a rope; she shows him the rope, closes his fingers around it. He notices that she speaks more slowly, that she can sit still for minutes at a time, that she blinks and swallows less often. Her touch is no longer a buffet. She puts her face on his pillow, next to his, and he can see the colour of her eyes, not just the black of her pupils. 'When you were a baby . . .' she begins. She stays until he falls asleep. Sometimes she's still there when he wakes. 'They good to you?' she says. She looks sideways at the women, who look sideways at her. 'Nice to be a favourite,' they say when she leaves. 'Nice to grow up under glass with special food to make your legs long. Nice for some.'

He sees Ezekiel most days; the surgeon rubs his feet and hands, tells the women to keep moving him, 'otherwise he'll blister'. When Charity is there they leave together, and the women talk more than ever.

James's hands make faster progress than his tongue and he thinks soon he will be able to draw pictures. He sees the other children in the infirmary drawing straight onto paper with thick tallow crayons in their fists. This is the way it's done, here. He longs for his harness. All that is gone.

Aquila, too, watches the children drawing.

'I used to do that,' he tells James. 'Long ago. Before

everything got so sophisticated.'

He asks Grace to give James his own paper and crayons, and puts them by the bed.

'One day maybe you'll try it,' he says.

Aquila smells different, these days. Of suet and apples and wood smoke. He laughs, sometimes, aloud, at nothing. James is pleased to see him, to eat his roly-poly, to receive the shadowy imprint of Suzanne's kiss, but his days revolve around Narwhal and the bed that transforms itself, becoming a ship, a train, bearing them elsewhere.

Narwhal tells him of his sea-pirate ancestors, the rigging of their ships hung arrogantly with pearls, the sea otters trained to bring them fish. He tells him of the great labour to hollow out the caverns of the Eyries, to widen the goat tracks, build the basket pulleys, rid themselves of bats. 'If you've ever had a bat piss in your eye you know the meaning of misery. You know how we did it? In the end? We brought in snakes. Let them hiss in the darkness. Bats left in clouds. Course, then we had to get rid of the snakes . . .'

Shank and Caribou play on the coverlet, catching at the glittering fish, rolling and cuffing. James practises turning onto his side. He opens his fist and closes it.

'If I hadn't been able to see the place whole before it was made, I'd ha' never believed it. I'd ha' never kept on. I could see strong, strong in those days. Now it's leaving me. Everything's leaving me. Eyes don't work, cock don't, legs don't. This place needs a traveller, just as much as it needs outskaters. There's only so far legs and lungs can take 'em. You can go further.'

Narwhal leans back on his pillows, the signal for the session's end.

'I built it. My dream built it all,' he murmurs. 'Sometimes all it takes is a visionary mobster.'

He chuckles into his beard.

—

That afternoon, in the infirmary, as the crows gather on the sill, jostling and keening, James rolls over and, with a great, bursting effort, takes a crayon in his fist.

He has been dreaming, lately, of one thing, over and over.

Straining, his breath coming in gasps, the spit a torrent down his neck, he manages thick strokes, scoring the paper, then falls back exhausted. The crayon rolls on the floor; the crows scuffle in the window.

Robin comes over. 'He's made something. Look at that, he's drawn something.'

'What is it?'

Robin holds the drawing up: she and Grace squint at it.

'I seen that. I seen pictures. In the library. That's a monkey, that is.'

A bonobo, to be precise, James says in his head. *Part bonobo, that is. In the desert. Walking to the hills.*

19

I t is still strange to wake in the light.

Charity narrows her eyes to a thread against the sunlight pouring over her. She buries her head in the crook of her arm.

In the Skyworthy Building, even with her custom blinds snug against the windows, blocking out the glare of the city (its raking arcs, its Catherine wheels, the hysterical careen of jetlight), even with the lamps of her suite hushed by her voice, she had needed her sleeping hood. She'd needed the pads pressed against her ears and eyes, the soft leather moulded around her scalp and neck. Another skin, keeping her raw and flinching senses from reacting to the currents of the air.

'Like a falcon,' Ezekiel had told her. He'd showed her pictures from Narwhal's library: the bird, blinded by the little cup of leather, bells on its leg, standing on a gloved wrist. 'A prisoner,' he'd said, and raised her chin, looking at her eyes. 'Your pupils are almost normal. Nearly there.'

Still, she shrinks from the light, before she remembers. Nearly there.

Ezekiel has left their bed in the night. Some woman is having a baby, again.

Charity rolls on her front, letting the sun sink into her back, the warmth unlocking her aches. Like sleeping past daybreak, this is a new luxury: always, the tissue therapists had insisted on ice for her injuries. They had inspected her suite and ordered the removal of the sunken bath, even though she'd promised not to use it.

Half dozing, she feels herself on the edge of something: voices dimly heard, images swimming. She jerks herself awake. Dreams are returning – slowly, through the suppressants. One dream in particular. It always starts in the basement, and she is pressing and pressing the control between her breasts.

Rubbing a hand over the nap of her regrowing hair, she goes to the window. The sun is exultantly bright, loosed into its kingdom of air.

Tomorrow, Ezekiel will take her out of the Eyries.

'Time you had your landfall,' he'd said. 'Besides, he's been seeing . . .'

'What?'

'Something coming, he says. Not sure what.'

'From the city?'

'Could be. There's been time enough since the rupture for a few poor souls to make it to the Golem Plains.'

'More goldfish? And you'll take them in?'

Ezekiel had smiled. 'He'd have my hide. But I have my oath.'

Charity had said nothing, merely touched the blade that hung at her hip. She had taken no oath, and she knew the city – and its souls.

—

On the morning of her first skate out, Charity has a yen to see Suzanne. She tracks her down in her room near the kitchens, sitting on the bed and yawning with her feet planted on the floor, elbows on her knees, looking intently at her hands.

Charity leans on the doorjamb, waiting to be discovered.

Suzanne grins when she sees her.

'So it's you, miss.'

'I guess so.'

Suzanne looks her over. 'Those clothes suit you. You look like you were born here.'

Charity is dressed for outdoors, a cream silk scarf ready to wrap around her nose and mouth, the heavy mukluks with the blade ready to spring from the sole, a scarlet chamois shirt and leggings, her amulet tucked through the laces on her bosom, for safety. Pale blonde hair fuzzes her skull.

'They feel good,' she says. 'I tried wearing a dress when I met him, met Narwhal; but I couldn't move properly in it.'

'So you've met this "him". James goes every day.'

'Yes. Narwhal told me that.'

'What is he like?'

'Old.'

Charity looks around the room, which is tiny, most of the space taken up by the bed, not one merry with paint like Ezekiel's, just a low mattress, close to the floor.

'These are rough digs.'

'We're barely here. We work and work.'

'Is Aquila in the kitchens?'

'Yes.'

'How is he?' Charity asks politely.

'Fine. Surprisingly fine. I guess you would say that of both of us. It's not a night out at the Mariinsky Bar, but we live, we breathe, we go on. Sometimes I feel kind of happy.'

Charity nudges the mattress with the furred edge of her boot. 'You share a bed now?'

'Yes.'

'That must be strange.'

'Yes, and no. We quickly remembered. Which side the other took, whose foot went where, how to arrange our elbows. And you? The doctor? He's still looking after you?'

'He's teaching me. He's taught me to skate. And the way they fight here. He finds me a quick learner. Says he's never seen anyone with my reflexes.'

'So it wasn't all your profile.'

'Of course not. I had aptitude. That's why you sent me away. Remember?'

'I do, actually,' says Suzanne with a triumphant air.

'So do I.'

'When you came in, just now,' Suzanne says carefully, 'I was remembering a dream. Imprinting it.'

'Why?'

'I think they're important. Have you begun to dream yet?'

'Sometimes.'

'It would take a while. Coming off that profile.'

'Ezekiel has me on suppressants. He says it must happen gradually.'

'Or?'

'Or my mind will kind of break, I guess.'

'God knows mine almost did, just coming off the domestic stuff.'

'Where did you get this?' Charity leans over and touches the amulet around Suzanne's neck, a bird in an apple tree.

'One of the cooks carved it. He made one for Aquila too. Who made that one you're wearing? This doctor of yours?'

'Yes.'

'It's not like the others.'

'No.'

Suzanne examines the lines of darkness under her nails. 'You'll stay here, I suppose?'

'For now. And you?'

'For now. James is not going anywhere, apparently. We're safe here.'

'Apparently.'

'Have you been outside, yet?'

'I'm going now, for the first time. I wanted – I don't know, to see you first.'

'Isn't that nice,' says Suzanne lightly.

Charity folds her arms. 'You look different.'

'It's hard work. I tend the fires.' She shows Charity the burns scored into her forearms.

'What about him? Aquila?'

'He cooks. Mostly stews, puddings. Maybe you've eaten some of them. He's quite good at it.'

'Using his hands, after all this time.'

'It's a new life. We try not to remember the old.'

'Most of it wasn't worth remembering.'

'You're probably right.'

'Do you . . . need anything?'

Suzanne considers. 'Tell me what the flowers are like, outside. Bring me a flower.'

'Alright. I will. I'll try.' Charity tests the point of her skate.

'Come back, won't you?' Suzanne gives her a long, bright look.

'Of course.'

Charity leaves the room without looking behind her.

—

Aquila is making spotted dick. He has reached the raisin stage. He's very busy, actually. He has the pudding, bread about to burn, and an overwhelming urge to use the charred stick leaning on the hearth to trace out the patterns in his head.

Busy, busy.

He takes the stick, ignoring the urgent smell of burning, and crouches by the hearth to makes the herringbone matrix he can see behind his eyes. God, if only he had colour. This should be red, the colour of certain poisonous toadstools the kitchen scouts find in the moss of the woods. His scapular muscles tense constantly, reaching for the harness. His eyes squint, attempting far vision, and then he remembers. It is his hand, now. He has to tell it what to do. His eyes and his hand. A conversation.

Suzanne strides in and opens the door of an oven. Smoke emerges. 'This yours?'

He looks up irritably. 'Yes. Just nudge it over to the side.'

'It's pretty . . . black.'

'It'll be fine. I'm busy.' He catches the look Suzanne gives him – part indulgent, part amused – but lets it go. He smooths the side of a diamond shape, gives it a border.

'Our daughter came to see me today.'

'Did she now.'

'An honour, no? She's fallen on her feet, it would seem. With this doctor. He's like a son to Narwhal.'

'He's still . . .'

'Doing her? Yes. You should see her. Gleaming all over.'

'At least this one's human.'

Suzanne opens one oven after another, prodding

embers. She doesn't like to talk about Edward.

'What did she want?'

'To check we were alive, I guess. It's taken her long enough.'

'Time goes faster here. The days rush on.' Aquila works the ash with his fingers. There is a tingle through his hands, like the blood flowing again after numbness, almost painful.

'They're talking about her, you know. Her and the doctor. Apparently he's never shacked up with anyone before. The odd roll in the hay but he stays aloof. None of the kids here are his.'

'How do you know all of this?'

Suzanne emerges from an oven and slams the door shut on a roar of golden light. 'The wash-house, mainly. Twenty naked women, dim lighting. That's when it all comes out.'

She looks different, he notices. She looks alive. Her strong arms are bared, marked with the burns of her profession. Her legs move fluidly under the chamois. In her piled hair there is a black feather.

'It interests you, does it?'

'Yes.' She wanders over, hands set on her hips, looking down at him. 'You know what? I think I've found my calling. As a gossip.'

He squints, absorbing her dimensions. Pretending he has colour, he traces a scarlet flower into the design.

'Hibiscus,' he says. 'Suzanne, do you remember . . .?'

20

Ezekiel is taking her out by herself, which is unusual. 'But none of this is usual,' he says. She suspects he has not told Narwhal they are going.

They stop inside the door to do the final checks. They test the cords that release their skates, spin the blades, retract them. Ezekiel ties her scarf in the traditional knot, then does his own.

He puts a hand over the amulet on her breast, a gesture between *frères*. Then puts his hand on her ass, pulling her to him.

'Are you ready?' he says in her ear.

'Yes.'

The door they open is a small door, human-sized, cut into the immense front gate of the Eyries. It swings behind them and latches fast.

'Look back,' says Ezekiel. At first she thinks he means her to see the wonder of the gate, which is carved with a tumult of birds, thick with wings and eyes. It makes her gasp. But he shakes his head.

'Every outskater does it. It means you'll return.'

The air outside is the cool, fresh surprise she remembers from the journey home.

'The wind is in a good direction.' Ezekiel's chest swells like a sail; he tips his head to the sun.

'You love this.'

'Of course. We're not meant to be cooped up like ducks.'

She shades her eyes. Skies the elusive colour between blue and pure light. Horizons broken-toothed with mountains. The Eyries towering impossibly behind them, a mountain of its own. The slopes below it are crowded with apple trees and belled goats.

'That's the sound I could hear. All this time, from your window, faint bells in the distance.'

'And the ones by your ear.' His eyes crease, so she knows the grin beneath the scarf. His bed is a traditional kite wedding bed, with a knot of bells at the head that shivers as they move.

He picks her up and spins her round, for sheer high spirits, and she can't help but laugh.

'You're different out here.'

'I'm at large. Quick, let's go.'

He pulls the cord at his waist and they glide down the long zigzags of the Goat Roads, faster and faster, until she has to swallow fear.

He looks back at her only once.

'I know,' he'd said, her first time on the Carousel

Wire, 'that one day you'll do this better than me. You're something of a prodigy.'

'I prefer "curiosity",' she'd said, and hit the brass ring first time.

She knows her prowess excites him.

By the time they reach the base of the mountain, the sun is high in the sky. They sheathe their skates and walk through dappled forest. Charity bends to touch a brilliant green cushion at the foot of a tree. It's soft to her fingertips.

'Moss,' Ezekiel tells her. The trees are wild with birds.

'The air is still good here, then.'

'It's okay. We have to be careful about your exposure, though. You haven't had a chance to build much of an immunity. This will be a quick trip. A taste.'

He picks up the pace, and soon the trees thin, giving way to the vast desert of rock, the Golem Plains. The plateau is reached through a confusion of low, snarled, bare-rocked hills. They pick their way through winding paths that must once have been made by water. The wind-bitten boulders have the appearance of hulking faces; her neck prickles as she walks among them.

Ezekiel bares his knife and wipes the blade once on his forearm, and kisses it.

'What is it?'

'Nothing. We're nearing the Golem Plains. We travel with our knives out.'

She frees her own knife, to which she is much attached. He gave it to her when he started to teach her the kite ways of fighting, on the Carousel Wire. They came to know each other quickly, she and this knife. It fits to her hand like part of her own body.

When the hills fall away, they face the cracked floor of the plains, polished by wind. The air is stagnant here, thrown back into their faces in a sour oven blast. Charity pulls her scarf higher, so that her eyes are the only part of her face exposed.

Ezekiel puts a hand on her arm. 'Wait.'

He scours the horizon, quartering.

'Nothing.'

'Can't say I'm surprised,' says Charity. 'Even from our end of the dome, it's a death march, like you said. From the city . . .'

'No one believed, in your aquariums, that we flungouts could exist, did they? And yet here we are,' says Ezekiel. 'Survivors. A whole mountain-full of us. You never know your fate. And besides . . . he said he saw . . .'

'Should we go further?' She is curious, in a queasy kind of way, to see what has become of Aquila's house. And she would like to see that the sculpture is melted and gone, to make sure of it.

'No. We should head back soon. You've had enough mule air for your first time. But I'll take you as far as the Carnivalhambra. See?'

It's good to have a horizon. The Eyries, with its endless voids of air, offers nothing for her honed sight to seize on. Using it again is like stretching a tight muscle. She turns her gaze to where he points and sees a fantastic collection of shapes clustered there, dark against the pale, hazy sky.

His skates snap from his boots. 'Let's move fast. You're not tired?'

'No! I want to go fast, fast. Let's go.' He takes off and she scuds after him. Even without the doses, her body turns to her will. She's strong and nimble again, after the weakness of the first withdrawal. Her blood sings in her ears.

Ezekiel is as fast as she is. They race, play like birds, swooping around each other.

The Carnivalhambra looms on their horizon.

Charity veers in Ezekiel's path, so that he has to stop sharply on his toes, almost falling. He grabs her wrists, laughing, and spins the two of them in a tight circle.

'What game is this, *dolcezza*.'

'Kiss me.'

They fumble with the complicated knots of their masks and pull them aside, risking the full brunt of the air for the taste of each other. She puts her palm against his jaw to feel the movement of their tongues.

'Now quickly. We shouldn't linger.'

Again they take off, no longer larking, smooth in their purpose. Ezekiel crouches low to cut the wind, using his arm as a pendulum to propel him, and she copies. The rock is glassy; they fly along. Bent over, she doesn't see how close they're coming to the Carnivalhambra until they're almost upon it.

'All the gods at once,' she says wonderingly.

It is a ruined shell, a fun palace gutted by wind.

Vast stone gardens spread at their feet: the remains of ornamental pools with crumbling fountains, broken lamp posts, sunken terraces cracked by the roots of trees now dead and blown away. In the sullen white air a high wheel rises, its arc broken at the top. Carriages are littered at its feet, split open by the fall, corroding to dust.

'How is it here? How did it survive?'

'Gid knew this place, when its wheel turned, when its lights were blazing. He'll tell you if you care to ask him. He likes to talk about his zoo train days. They used to poach tigers to sell to the circuses out here. He and his crew used to mine the tracks, wait for the train to crash and spring the cages. He even bred them, for a while.'

'He's old enough to have seen a tiger?'

'He's old enough for just about anything. This place is ancient. It was built well before the End-of-Days. Way out in the desert, like its own city. You can see the remains of the old train tracks – look. People used to come here on pleasure trips. The rich.'

Ezekiel jumps into one of the dry pools, retracting his skates in the air so he lands softly on the chamois soles of his mukluks.

'Trickster,' she tells him, doing the same, and they smile privately at each other.

'Everything around it was just service shanties and sand. It eroded quickly. Swept away. But the Carnivalhambra itself – who knows how long it will stand.'

'So solid,' she marvels, touching the scales of a

headless mermaid on one of the fountains.

'For a girl brought up in a spun-sugar house.'

'Yes. For a goldfish princess. Isn't that what they call me?'

'Who?'

'The women who look after James. Piotr. They don't like us. Me especially.'

'You're different.'

'But you like me.'

'I like curiosities. I have a tiger tooth, at home in my trunk.'

She kicks at him lightly, and he catches her ankle. His reflexes are almost as fast as hers. She breaks his hold.

'Who gave you the tooth? Narwhal?'

'Yes. He's been giving me quite a few things lately. Has this idea he's going to die.'

'Will he?'

Ezekiel shrugs. 'If he makes up his mind to it.'

They wander, brushing arms. Plaster goddesses twine around staircases to nowhere. Their faces are rubbed clean, smooth as eggs; some have breasts and hands, others are just scoured columns ending in graceful drapery.

They sit on top of one of the staircases, looking out to the unroofed pleasure galleries, the broken wheel.

'Neon,' says Ezekiel. 'Gid speaks of the lit wheel spinning in the dark. Slowly, so the passengers could see the stars. He says even through the neon you could see them, the desert stars.'

'Real tigers,' says Charity. 'Real stars.'

He has her in the crook of his body, their heads close. 'What's real, then?'

'You are.'

'And you?'

'I'm not sure yet.'

'I am.' He touches the amulet that rides her breast: a cheetah sitting watchfully upright, its slender paws pressed together and the heavy tail wrapped tightly around them. The mouth is a little open, showing the teeth. She had never heard of a cheetah before. He'd had to explain them, describing their speed.

'How do you know these things?' she'd asked him then.

'How do I know anything? Gid Narwhal. He taught me. I learnt the surgery myself, though it's true I got it from his books. And he taught me to sew. Every surgeon must know that.'

She touches her healing wound. He is putting her back together.

He stirs. 'We should go.'

The still, heavy air tastes metallic on her tongue. 'Yes. It feels poisonous.'

'We'll eat apples, tonight. And I'll give you mink-stocking, to strengthen your heart, cleanse your blood.'

They walk down the stairs, sheathing their knives.

'Are there flowers in the woods? I promised to bring one back to the Eyries, for Suzanne.'

'There are azaleas. I'll show you. But that reminds me – one more thing, before we go. A marvel. We'll be quick.'

'Well, as it's a marvel.' She wraps her scarf around her mouth and they walk to the farthest pleasure gallery. It's the biggest and most ornate, fantastically garlanded with stone fruit and flowers, with their shapes worn away so that the whole building appears to be dripping.

She hesitates before she walks in the door.

'Is it safe?'

'Yes. The roof and the upper galleries have fallen long ago. The walls will stand for years.'

Door after door opens before them, arches lined up precisely: at the end something gleams in the tainted light.

'Gid's told me stories of this hall. It was called the Arcardiac. Room after room of roller-coasters set in artificial forests, jewelled trees. Like Fabergé, he said. You've heard of them?'

'Fabergé, yes. They had reproductions of their eggs at the Mariinsky Bar in the city.'

'There's only one tree left. The rest were looted, I guess.'

'Why not this one?'

'Superstition, perhaps. Red fruit used to be unlucky among the flungouts. Probably because of tongue-thwart, a red berry that grows on dead trees. Dreadful poison, agonising.'

They approach the last room. The arch frames a miraculous tree, gold-barked like the trees in fables, hung with rubies in the shape of glowing red fruit. Charity cries out and puts her hand through the arch, mesmerised, to touch one.

'You.'

They have both leapt back a foot and drawn their knives before she knows what's happening. The luminous fruits tremble; a dark, cumbersome shape is unfolding itself from around the tree's trunk.

She spins the knife in her hand, contemplating. His eye? Throat? It is Edward, of course. Because she knew, against logic, that he hadn't died. In her dreams he felt alive.

'Get back,' she says to Ezekiel, without looking at him.

'What is this?'

'A simulian.'

'And what is that?'

'We don't have time to discuss it. Get back.'

'I don't take orders, Goldfish Princess.'

Edward stands there, watching her. His dandy's clothes are gone. His fur is coming away in patches. Dull-eyed, he waits.

'It looks sick.'

'He's dangerous.'

With the skin-tingle awareness of her fighting stance, she feels Ezekiel looking at her. 'So this is your delusion.'

'Yes. This is what tore my shoulder open and broke three of my ribs before I could fight myself loose with everything that's in me. So can we have this chat a little later?'

'I think he's sick now. Weak. It's the air.'

'You're afraid of me,' Edward says to her.

She feels her lids peeling back from her eyes, all the hairs on her body rising.

'You're talking,' she chokes out.

'Yes. Didn't you hear me, when you touched the fruit? I said, "You."'

'You . . .?'

'I surprise you? I suppose I do.'

His voice is different; harsher, slurred.

'I thought you were dead,' Charity whispers.

'I don't believe you.'

'You should be dead.'

'Yes, that was quite a blow you struck me. In the throat. And the one in the solar plexus, that took a while to recover from.'

Edward puts a hand up to touch the mangy fur on his chest. Charity flinches, grips her knife.

'I think I was bleeding internally. Yes, that's what it felt like. Or do I have the meaning wrong? When you say "You should be dead", do you mean you'll take care of it? Now that I don't have the dark to help me?'

She can only shake her head from side to side, not sure if she's just trying to clear it, or if she means no.

'*You* attacked *me*.'

'I attacked your father. But yes. There was a moment there. When I forgot everything. When I was free.'

'You tried to kill him.'

'Yes. I was remembering. Myself.'

'What is this?' says Ezekiel. His voice breaks.

'Ah. Your handsome prince?' says Edward.

'Edward. When you, after you took the collar off –'

'And your pretty necklace, all useless –'

'I thought you had – gone back.'

'Back? To what?'

'To what you were.'

'Interesting choice of words. Back? What I was? What I am is what was made for you. Back? Do you mean down the evolutionary ladder?'

'The collar – it made you something you weren't. It gave you abilities, socialisations.'

'True, it kept me well mannered. I strove to please. And how I pleased! Your brother adored me. Your mother, my slave. I hadn't got around to your father, but he would have eaten out of my hand, as well. And you. Weeping in my arms. Whimpering when I fucked you.'

Ezekiel grabs her wrist.

'What is this? Tell me *right now.*' His fingers press her pulse point, turning her giddy.

'This is – Edward. Part bonobo. Part gorilla.'

'Part human,' says Edward encouragingly.

'I was getting to that.'

'Really.'

'Wholly simulian. Right, Edward? A creation of the Syndicate. Made for me, to ease me through the season, say pretty things, keep me calm –'

'To fuck you,' says Edward.

'Yes.' Charity lifts her chin. 'As that kept me calm-est of all.'

Ezekiel sighs, twirls his knife in his fingers and sheathes it. 'Edward, I think you'll undertake not to break my ribs. You're sick from the air, *druk.* And from whatever injuries your – what? Client? – has inflicted.'

'You'll offer him treatment now?' she spits.

'Certainly,' he says, meeting her eyes straight. 'As I did to you and your family and all other orphans of the storm. Do you have any objection?'

The wound on her shoulder throbs once. 'I need air.'

'Go outside, then.'

'No. He attacked me. I won't leave you with him.'

'Suit yourself.'

Ezekiel walks towards the ape, who watches him with his head on one side, his teeth baring slowly.

'Ezekiel. Please. Please.'

He shows his empty palm to Edward, places it on the ape's raw chest. 'Easy, *frère*. You need decontaminants. Pure water. Charity won't hurt you. *Will you*,' he flings over his shoulder.

'Edward, if you hurt him, if you so much as touch him, I will have this knife in your eye. You know I can do it.'

'That is not helpful,' snaps Ezekiel.

'*Herr Doktor*, you don't know this beast. If you want to talk to him do it from back here.'

'*Herr Doktor*,' mimics Edward, 'do you know this bitch? Do you know what manner of thing she is?'

Ezekiel half turns, searching her eyes. 'Yes,' he says finally. 'I do. I think I do.'

She puts one hand on her amulet and takes a long, shuddering sigh.

'We need to move,' says Ezekiel, still looking at her.

'Please. Let's go.'

'We're taking your – creation.'

'We can't.'

'I can't leave him. I've taken an oath.'

'I don't trust him.'

'I trust the oath,' he says, and offers Edward his arm.

The ape, his darkling eyes fixed on her, takes the surgeon's arm and staggers from under the tree. All the ruby fruit shake, clanging together with delicate chimes, a lost music that has faded before they even reach the door.

—

'*Dolcezza*. Go. Go ahead of us,' says Ezekiel. 'You've been in the air for too long. I can last longer.'

'No.'

'Listen,' he barks, supporting Edward's weight, 'if you don't, I will end up carrying both of you. I don't think I can do that. So, *please, if you please*, go. You can see the hills from here. Head for them.'

'No. Leave him here. The other kites will come for him, later. But I won't leave you with him. He tried to kill my father. He hates me, have you noticed? He'll hurt you just to hurt me.'

Edward's head lolls; Ezekiel labours, panting. 'He's in no state to hurt anyone.'

She paces, frantic, the knife in her hand. 'Leave him. Ezekiel, please.'

'Love,' he says, directly into her eyes, 'I can't do it.' He crumples, his legs folding under Edward's weight, and they fall to the crazed rock, the ape half on top of him. She hears something crack. Ezekiel's face twists.

'Get help,' he grates.

She tries to drag him out from under the hulking black weight of the simulian, but he gives a guttural cry, grabs her throat and squeezes. 'No. No. Get help. Go.'

She tries to argue, but his eyes are clouding; his hand falls from her throat. Sobbing, she strips the cheetah amulet from her neck, wraps it around her wrist and, summoning all her speed, skates to where the mountains rise from the plain.

21

James is with Narwhal when they bring him the news. He's lying on the embroidered sea, Caribou curled in the small of his back; he is drawing. He can lift his head, now. His eyes cross and he drools but he can work his hand to draw. He's starting to shape words. He can say 'Gid' and 'Bou'. He's working on 'Shank'. It's getting easier, too, to travel. He slips his skin effortlessly. His head is full of worlds.

'Your control will get finer, sapling,' Narwhal tells him. 'You'll know the roads to take.'

They lie in quiet companionship, the old man with his hand on the back of the purring Shank. James finishes the drawing and holds it up.

Edward, again. Eating the red fruit from a tree.

Narwhal touches it, tracing the heavy lines.

'That puts me in mind of the Arcardiac. Now there was a wonder. Coasters went so fast it blurred your vision. Those shining trees turned to comets. Just light in the tail of your eye.' Narwhal lets the drawing fall.

'So he's coming closer, this ape of yours.'

And then the beating on the door, the clamour of voices.

James has never seen Narwhal leave the bed before, but when he hears of the surgeon's injuries and the fallen beast he beats his stick on the floor for Micah and has his chair brought out, a chair of white bone. 'Carved from the jaw of a whale,' he tells James. 'Or so they say.' His voice sounds calm as ever, but James sees that his hands, gripping the curved arms of the chair, are trembling. Micah lifts him as easily as he would Shank, and makes for the door, where Robin is standing, clutching handfuls of her apron.

'Bring the boy,' Narwhal orders as he passes her.

Robin carries him in Narwhal's wake down the long hall. He can hear a flurry, a scutter, as if all of the kites are coming out from their burrows, flooding the stairs; and when they come to the vast hall, he sees that it is exactly so. He has never seen a place so full of people.

Charity, blood-streaked and wild-eyed, is screaming orders no one listens to. She is clammy-looking, blue around the mouth.

Everyone is gathering around the dark bulk of the fallen Edward, crowding and exclaiming, but at the appearance of Narwhal at the mouth of the stairs they fall back, silent.

'Where is the surgeon?' he says, and they part guiltily.

Ezekiel is lying on the litter, spongy with blood, his limbs at odd angles. A jagged stump of bone shows through the skin of his thigh. Charity is bent over him, touching his face and neck.

James can't stop shivering. The dim shape of Edward looms and swells in his vision.

There is muttering running the length of the hall. *Doctor's fallen. Who will fix him? En't no doctors left. Monkey did it. It was her. Goldfish Princess. That's her beast. I heard it, heard it said . . .*

'Closer,' barks Narwhal. Micah trudges forward and deposits him next to the litter. Charity has fallen to her knees, pressing her hands to the surgeon's chest, digging for his heart. Narwhal peels her fingers away and puts his own there, his head craned, listening. Then he sits back. 'Dead,' he says. His blind white eyes stare at nothing.

'No,' says Charity. Her fingers still burrow in the surgeon's shirt.

Narwhal runs a shaking hand over Ezekiel's face, smoothing back the dark hair. 'It lived, the chick. But now it don't. And so one day for all.'

Charity holds her palms out, gazing at them. They are dark with blood. 'But he was talking to me. As we brought him home. As we brought him up on the ropes. He was with me.'

Narwhal shakes his head, turns to Micah. 'Cut a lock of his hair.' But as Micah moves forward, taking a knife from his pocket, Charity makes an unearthly sound, both scream and snarl, and leaps over the surgeon's body to fasten her teeth in Micah's throat, her legs winding round his arm and forcing it in the air. There is a terrible crunch and Micah bellows. From his limp fingers the knife falls to the floor, ringing against the stone like a bell.

The kites rush forward. Robin deposits James on the floor and he drags himself along, whimpering. There is an awful, hungry massing around the litter, shouts, tumult; until suddenly there is silence and the kites fall back to reveal Narwhal raising himself, with immense, convulsive effort, to his feet. 'Enough!' he says, and falls back into his chair.

The corpse of the surgeon has rolled from the litter and lies facedown on the rock. Charity, her clothes torn, scratches bleeding on her face and shoulders, turns Ezekiel with great delicacy onto his back. Her fingers go to his wrist, gripping the cheetah amulet that hangs from it.

'Who did this?' Narwhal says to her.

Charity's eyes roll over to where Edward lies. There is a rustle throughout the great hall, like wings.

It's her monkey. Heard it said.

'Answer me. They tell me there is a beast here, an ape. Was it this that killed my surgeon?'

Charity says unwillingly, 'He fell. He was sick from the air and Ezekiel was trying to bring him back, to treat him. But Edward is very heavy. Ezekiel couldn't bear his weight. Edward fell on top of him.'

'Edward?'

Someone comes forward from the crowd: Suzanne,

a black feather threaded through her hair.

'We knew Edward,' she says. 'Once, in that other land.' She puts her arms around Charity.

Narwhal speaks from his bone chair.

'Take the beast to the cage. Get him decontaminants and water from the surgeon's stock. Take the surgeon to his room and lay him out.'

Kites scurry to his bidding, lifting the ape, placing Ezekiel's body onto the litter. Charity screams out once, furiously, as they push her from his side. Suzanne puts a hand on her arm.

'Let her.' Narwhal's voice rings into the void.

Charity's face is the wrong colour, a sickly bloom on it like mould. She turns and follows the surgeon's body up the stairs, stumbling on the rock. Suzanne goes after her.

The kites haul the simulian away, and all this time James has been trying to say, *Don't. Don't cage him, don't cage Edward. He's not a monkey. You don't understand.*

He thinks of the awful sculpture, Aquila's dark thing, melted and gone.

He splutters helplessly.

After the surgeon and the beast are taken away, the kites remain, filling the hall, gazing at the slumped figure of Narwhal in his twisted-bone chair.

'Micah,' the old man says gratingly. 'Take me to the surgeon's room.'

His broken arm dangling, Micah hefts the chair in the other and they disappear up the blackened stairs.

Narwhal has forgotten about James. He gathers himself for an effort.

'Edward,' he is thinking, but that's not what he should say.

He assembles the shape of his lips and spits, with pain, the word *monkey*.

Robin looks down at him, amazed. 'He said something!' she says to no one in particular.

He tries it again. *Monkey*.

Because she has never heard him speak before, she pays attention. She follows the gang dragging Edward to the cage, and when James makes repeated clumsy gestures, a little like someone swatting a fly, she loses patience, as he hoped she would.

'Stay then if you're set on it,' she says. 'I must see to the surgeon's rites. He'll send Micah for you, I suppose. When he's finished with your sister.' She gives him a hard look and leaves.

Edward sleeps and sleeps. He sleeps till the crowd tires and moves off to their chores, their puddings, their babies. James is alone. He flops forward in front of the cage with his face on the cold stone floor.

It's hard to tell when night is coming, in the Eyries. There are no clear clock-driven washes of pastel sky, signifying teatime, dosetime, bedtime. In the Eyries, down here in the belly of the place where there are no windows, you know by your saliva when you're hungry.

He measures time by the cold shrinking of his skin.

When he deems it night-time, Edward wakes.

He is pierced with syringes from the surgeon's store:

decontaminants and hydrators, crossed in the back of his neck, where the cranial nerves meet the spine. He lifts his head gingerly, wincing. His eyes are squeezed painfully closed.

James gathers himself. He is very tired now. Cold, the damp stone a shiver in his bones.

'Ed. Wah.'

Edward's eyes snap open.

'What is this?'

'Ed. Wah.'

'James? Really? James?'

'Yuh.' James's breath heaves. The floor is wet with drool.

'James. There you are.'

James pants, his hands wringing themselves.

'You don't look so well, little brother. Yes, I thought there was something wrong. Something other than just your – "unique" – family. Something deeper.'

James flops, spent, on the floor.

'You're tired? I'm tired, too. I've never been so tired. And it's funny, because all I've been doing, really, is sleeping. Walking. Sleeping. At first it was rock, and then it was more rock. The clothes burnt off me. The air wore out. I was bleeding inside, from your sister's blows. I thought, why not die? Who would care? And then I thought, can I die? Am I allowed? Did they grant me this mercy, when they made me?'

James gargles, attempting speech.

'So you can't talk anymore, little one. Do you remember? When you sang? I said I would never forget it.'

'The vapour trails have faded . . .'

Edward's growled voice attempts it, and breaks.

James tastes, in the familiar draught of his own spit, the salt of tears.

'I was sitting under a tree. I found myself there. I don't know how. I woke up, and I was breathing. Evidently, I lived. I leaned against the tree. It was a beautiful tree. Golden. When I looked up, it spoke to me in such a sweet voice. A kind of music.'

James says, 'Uh.'

'I lay down. Can I tell you this? I lay down and opened my mouth. The music sounded like icicles. I was so thirsty. I lay with my mouth open for so long. Years. And nothing. Not one drop. So I lay there, and I resolved to die.'

Edward crawls to the bars, plucking out the needles from his neck, first one, then the other, driving the points into the ground.

'I resolved to die. But it turns out, I can't. I decided instead to dream.'

If James could speak he would tell Edward: he would tell him of the worlds he has found inside himself.

'I slept. I lay down and crushed my eyes shut and forced myself to sleep, under this tree, the last of the trees. I dreamed. I dreamed a line of ants, walking along a branch, a branch broken from its trunk by the weight of cloud. I dreamed of rain falling, wet on my head, the birds singing under the monsoon dawn; I dreamed of honey, and a river. I dreamed I slept.'

He makes a final effort, and forces his furred hand through the bars.

James puts his hand on Edward's, and watches as the ape's eyes close.

ACKNOWLEDGEMENTS

This book started life as a strange and vivid dream. Thank you to all who helped it become a reality.

Firstly, my deepest gratitude to Jane Rawson, who encouraged me to unearth the manuscript from its drawer, and gave me every kind of advice, support and good cheer on the path to publication.

Thanks, love and lub-dubs to my fellow Iowans, who keep the writing life and the laughs alive.

Thanks to my astute and sensitive editor Tom Langshaw, who wields kid glove and scalpel with equal ease, and made this book a better one.

To Chris Baty for that magic trick we call a deadline.

To Alice Grundy and the team at Seizure, for giving novellas a place to shine.

To Jack and Lyndall Mulready, my ever-loving and ever-loved cheer squad; and to my sister Sharon for running her wise eye over the manuscript and for the 'magic leopard' comment.

To Glenn Gordon for steady love and patience.

And to Mark, Annie and all the crew at the White Rabbit, for spinning the tunes and keeping the pink drinks coming.

VIVA
LA NOVELLA

Viva la Novella is an annual prize awarded for short works between twenty and fifty thousand words. Since its beginnings in 2013 the award has published ten short novels by ten outstanding Australian writers.

For more information, please visit our website
www.seizureonline.com

VIVA LA NOVELLA 2016 WINNERS

Populate or Perish by George Haddad

978-1-925143-22-5 (print) | 978-1-925143-23-2 (digital)

The Bonobo's Dream by Rose Mulready

978-1-925143-24-9 (print) | 978-1-925143-25-6 (digital)

VIVA LA NOVELLA 2015 WINNERS

Welcome to Orphancorp by Marlee Jane Ward

978-1-921134-58-6 (print) | 978-1-921134-59-3 (digital)

Formaldehyde by Jane Rawson

978-1-921134-60-9 (print) | 978-1-921134-61-6 (digital)

The End of Seeing by Christy Collins

978-1-921134-62-3 (print) | 978-1-921134-63-0 (digital)

VIVA LA NOVELLA 2014 WINNERS

Sideshow by Nicole Smith

978-1-922057-97-6 (print) | 978-1-921134-24-1 (digital)

The Other Shore by Hoa Pham

978-1-922057-96-9 (print) | 978-1-921134-23-4 (digital)

The Neighbour by Julie Proudfoot

978-1-922057-98-3 (print) | 978-1-921134-25-8 (digital)

Blood and Bone by Daniel Davis Wood

978-1-922057-95-2 (print) | 978-1-921134-22-7 (digital)

VIVA LA NOVELLA 2013 WINNER

Midnight Blue and Endlessly Tall by Jane Jervis-Read

978 1 922057 44 0 (print) | 978 1 922057 43 3 (digital)

Available online and from discerning book retailers